Ellie and the Prince

FARAWAY CASTLE

J. M. STENGL

To Hannah C., aka "Ariel," first official fan of
Ellie and Omar, encourager, and friend.
Blessings on your own writing journey.

CHAPTER ONE

LLIE HAD JUST ENTERED THE CASTLE LOBBY when her wristband pager sent a tingle of magic up her arm. She checked it then hurried over to Faraway Castle Resort's front desk. "I'm here, Sten. What's going on?"

The dwarf perched atop a stool behind the desk looked up from his own wristband in surprise and beamed his friendly smile. "Good morning! Glad I caught you before you left the building. A hobgoblin just tried to steal a cake from the kitchen. The brownies snagged him."

A minor event. Ellie relaxed. "Geraldo, no doubt. Did the cake survive?"

Sten's eyes twinkled. "Sounds like it escaped

injury, but a few of the brownies got scratched." Sten, like all dwarfs working at the castle, wore a glamour that made him appear human to unmagical guests. Ellie barely noticed the glamour. Her friend was middle-aged with gray in his beard, but his dark eyes were bright and young.

"This shouldn't take long. See you later!" She pushed away from the desk, took a service elevator down to the basement, and entered the huge kitchen, where brownies swarmed in a flurry of breakfast clean-up and lunch preparation. Despite their frenzied labor, not a speck of dirt marred the flagstone floor, and delicious scents wafted to Ellie's nose. Dark wooden beams supported the kitchen's low ceiling, and half a pig roasted over the huge open fireplace. It might have been a scene from centuries past but for the gleaming cookstoves, stainless-steel sinks, granite countertops, and a restaurant-quality dishwasher. Here the brownies produced fine cuisine for large crowds of discriminating resort guests three times a day. Magic was decidedly involved. The room fairly buzzed with it.

"Is Geraldo here?" Ellie asked a passing chef.

The brownie looked way up at her, his dark eyes huge in his small face. "They chased him up to the dining hall, ma'am. Our cake survived the attack."

Ellie nodded, trying not to smile. "I'm glad to hear it." To a brownie, the loss of a cake to a hobgoblin would be akin to murder. No matter if the sweet was created only to be eaten; hobgoblins had no right to any dessert intended for castle guests.

She hurried up the back service stairs and entered the formal dining hall directly. Sunlight angled through a bank of windows facing the lake, glinting off the polished silver coffee set on a side table. No guests were present, but brownies scurried about, already laying fresh tablecloths and setting tables for the noon meal. Near the dumbwaiter she spotted Geraldo, his spindly arms held fast by a brownie on each side.

"Thanks for waiting patiently," Ellie addressed the brownies. "I'll take care of him now."

They released Geraldo, bowed respectfully, and returned to their regular duties. Brownies seldom smiled, yet they were cheery creatures who delighted in housework of all kinds. Ellie couldn't comprehend the appeal of menial labor, but she was grateful. Who wouldn't appreciate such diligent, flawless service?

Geraldo hunched, arms crossed over his chest.

Ellie sat cross-legged on the parquet floor and focused on the scowling hobgoblin, ignoring the quiet bustle around them. "I'm disappointed, Geraldo. You know very well that guests will drop plenty of cake crumbs on the floor after dinner this evening," she said. "The children never fail you."

His scowl deepened. "Crumbs, pah!"

"You are ten inches tall. You don't need an entire cake."

"I want it anyway," he mumbled. Although wizened, toothless, and unimaginably old, Geraldo thought and behaved like a child. When Ellie first arrived at the castle six years ago, the scowling, grouchy hobgoblins had frightened her, but before long she'd realized their dramatics were only for show. The silly creatures insisted on wearing colorless rags no matter how many new garments they were offered, all for the sake of claiming ill-treatment.

She focused on producing a calm, soothing

tone. "I don't want to call for the Gamekeeper, but I shall have to if you start stealing entire cakes. The director will insist on it, and what a shame that would be!" She didn't have to fake sincerity, for she was fond of the grouchy hobgoblin despite his sulks and threats. "Please try to be content with the crumbs that fall tonight. We have many active and messy children with us this month, you know."

He nodded grudgingly. "Very well. I'll wait for my cake. But if no crumbs fall tonight, I make no promises about tomorrow." He glared up at her over his long, hooked nose. "You can stop bewitching me with that voice of yours, missy."

"Speaking of children," a shrill voice interrupted, "I must tell you something important, Miss Ellie."

She turned to see a slim brownie in a maid uniform gazing up at her. Even seated on the floor, Ellie loomed over the brownies and hobgoblins. "What is it, Sira?"

Sira twisted her apron between long-fingered hands and bobbed a curtsy before speaking. "Just now, some of us saw the Zeidan children sneak cinder sprites into the castle and head upstairs.

Their nanny was nowhere in sight, and the royal parents are at a lecture today. I would have tried to stop them, but you know how angry Madame Director is if we brownies show ourselves to guests, even children!"

"How many sprites?" Ellie asked, already rising and prepared to run.

Sira shrugged her tiny shoulders. "Four or five? It was a whole litter, and the mother too."

"Did they seem frightened?"

"They were squeaking. Oh, and Miss Ellie, you know Geraldo will try to steal another cake . . ."

Geraldo gave a "Harrumph" and slouched off to disappear under a table.

"Squeaking" was useless information; cinder sprites always squeaked. Ellie flashed Sira a quick grin anyway. "I do know, and thanks for the alert, Sira!" She checked her equipment pack and grimaced. Only three cages. She'd forgotten to restock. "I've got to run for more equipment. With any luck the sprites will remain calm, but if there is a fire alarm, please let Madame know I'm on my way."

Ellie sprinted from the castle to her small staff cottage, shoved a dozen of the one-inch glass-cube cages into her pack, then sprinted back to the castle. The weather was perfect—sunny, clear skies, a light breeze. She heard laughter and splashing from the lakeshore, the *thunk-thwack* of balls from the tennis courts, the distant whinny of a horse at the riding stables, and, laced through it all, the light hum of magic.

To be the official Controller of Magical Creatures at Faraway Castle—an exclusive resort for royal and noble guests from around the world—was a tremendous privilege, Ellie often reminded herself. Especially at her age, with her lack of magical training. But the Gamekeeper had appointed her, and not even the resort director dared overrule his decisions.

She entered the castle through a side door, charged up a set of service stairs, then hurried along a hall adorned with fine art pieces and crystal chandeliers, her footsteps muffled by thick carpeting. Rumor had it that Faraway Castle was once the palace of a great king. Ellie had no reason to doubt this story, for it retained much majestic beauty.

The royal suite in the castle's east wing, offering views of both the lake and the mountains, was currently occupied by the sovereigns of Khenifra, a kingdom located on a continent far to the south and reputed to be an important military power. This exceedingly handsome royal couple had produced numerous offspring who were, in Ellie's opinion, the most beautiful on earth.

The four youngest of these had accompanied their parents to the resort this year. "Lively" was the word most often used to describe them, a description usually spoken in fond tones but occasionally emitted through clenched teeth and a fake smile.

As soon as Ellie reached a large marble griffin and turned right, she heard muffled shouts and screams. She sprinted the last few yards then pounded on the suite's main door. When no answer came, she resorted to her passkey and rushed inside, puffing for breath. "Hello?" she called while pulling a cage cube, her spray bottle, and a scoop from her pack. She didn't yet smell smoke, but there was no time to lose.

"Little cinder sprites," she cooed softly. "Are any of you near me? I'm here to rescue you and take you to a quiet, beautiful place where you can eat sweet greens and run about without fear."

A soft, wistful squeak caught her ear. Going down on her knees, she peered under the ornately gilded hall table, saw a pair of shiny black eyes, and sensed the little beast's helpless dismay. "Hello, darling," she cooed. "You must be the mother. How did you end up here? Would you like my help? I promise to catch your babies and return them to you, but you need to let me capture you." Ellie continued to babble such reassurances, hardly paying attention to her words, for her tone was far more important.

The little creature made no objection as she reached in to pick it up. Not once did it brandish its sharp horns or show its long teeth. "You are a pretty mama," Ellie told it, stroking the soft hair that sprouted in all directions from its head and body. This sprite was white and red, and its tiny feet were pink. As soon as she felt its fright dissolve into trust, she tucked it into the cage, which magically expanded to a manageable yet comfortable size for the sprite and was already stocked with sprite food. The little creature immediately began munching on fresh greens.

Leaving that cage near the door, Ellie pulled several more from her pack and tucked them into her coverall pockets. These cages, blown from tempered glass to her exact specifications, were vital to her success. Cinder sprites, rare magical creatures native to these mountains, were adorable yet dangerous, for one frightened or angry sprite hiding under a pile of dry leaves or a sofa could start a raging fire in minutes. Ellie used her gift of soothing talk along with an herbal potion, her own recipe, to calm or quench the sprites as needed. Once isolated in tempered-glass cages they could safely be transported to a place less combustible than an ancient magical forest or castle.

"Hello?" she called, using her gift to calm humans and sprites alike as she followed the sound of voices to the sitting room.

"There it is! Catch it!" cried the eldest, a boy.

His sister grabbed for something under a chair but snatched her hands back with a cry. "It's too hot!" she cried. "You try. The rug is starting to burn!"

Ellie slid in between them on her knees and located a baby sprite that glowed red, snapping and crackling like a tiny bonfire. She quickly squeezed the trigger of her bottle to spray sweet-smelling liquid over the miniature inferno. The sprite collapsed into a steaming black puddle of goo.

"Is he dead?" the youngest child wailed.

"Oh no," Ellie said in her calmest tone. "I would never kill a sprite. The baby was so frightened that he might have turned straight to ash, so I extinguished him. He will recover once he dries out." She used her scoop to scrape the sprite from the rug and slide it into another expanding cage. The little girl sat beside the cage to make sure her sprite recovered. Her name was Rita, Ellie knew, having met the child as a tiny baby three summers ago.

She spent the next several minutes chasing down and capturing three more baby sprites and putting out small fires. One baby never did ignite, which made things easier. The children romped around, eager to help her find the terrified babies and fascinated to see how the cages grew to fit each furry inmate. Ellie used a second spray potion to clear the air and to repair the burned rug, a scorched chair leg, and a blistered shoe.

By the time the last creature was caged and the mess cleaned up, she was sweating and sooty but satisfied. She now knew the older three children by name: Princes Rafiq and Karim, ages twelve and five, and Princess Yasmine, age eight. She had seen them all around the castle many times over the years, watching them grow up without ever actually meeting them. They talked nonstop, usually all at once, which made communication a challenge, but she managed to calm them slightly and have brief conversation with each one individually. All four children captured her heart with their gorgeous dark eyes and brilliant smiles.

So very like their older brother Omar's.

But then, Ellie had long ago lost her heart to that brother, so this conquest was no surprise. If only he had come to the resort this summer! His family usually spent four weeks every June and July in this very suite to escape the summer heat of their homeland, but this year all five older children were occupied elsewhere. The heir to the throne was married, as was the eldest daughter, and the second son was recently betrothed, she knew from gossip.

But as far as she knew, Prince Omar was still unattached, and Ellie could never stop hoping that one of these summers . . . She had frequently met his steady gaze or encountered him in doorways, where he always politely opened the door for her and spoke a bashful word or two of greeting. Sometimes she even wondered if he might wish to become acquainted with her.

But this idea was completely ridiculous, for a prince must marry nobility or royalty; in many countries, royal children were betrothed at birth. Every summer she had seen Omar in the company of some beautiful princess or lady, though never the same one two years running and never with any evidence of romantic attachment. But his freedom couldn't last forever. For all Ellie knew, he was spending this holiday with his future wife's family in a distant country.

The temptation was strong to quiz these children about Omar, but she refused to use them in such a way. Glancing around, she noticed a distinct lack. "Where is your nanny?" she asked, pushing loose hair from her face. Her ponytail never seemed to last through a sprite hunt.

Yasmine went wide-eyed, but Rafiq brushed off the question. "We don't need her. I am old enough to watch over the little ones now."

"Are you?" Ellie wondered about this. But she

also knew that Madame Genevieve, the resort director, would never allow her magic-creature wrangler to fill in as a nanny, not even for royal guests. "I would feel more confident about your responsibility, Rafiq, if I didn't know that you helped bring these cinder sprites into your rooms," she said, giving him a level look.

He frowned and looked away, then shrugged and gave her a charming grin. "We won't do it again. How could we know they would light themselves on fire? Do they always do that?"

Ellie restrained a frustrated sigh. Guests were always warned about possible hazards, including sprites, but few seemed to pay attention.

"Only when they are frightened or angry," she told him. "But they are easily frightened, and some have hot tempers."

Rafiq and Yasmine chuckled. Rita kept a vigilant eye on her melted sprite, which was beginning to quiver in its cage. "Will he be all right?" she asked once more.

"He will be back to normal within the hour," Ellie assured her. "And hungry, so I'd better get him back to my cottage where I keep sprite snacks." She gave the little girl a wink. Rita lifted her arms, and Ellie caught her up for a big hug. Then Karim wanted a hug, and even Yasmine waited in line. Only Rafiq held out, considering himself far too old for such things.

Rafiq and Yasmine helped carry the cages and her pack to the door while the little ones bounced along behind. Just as Ellie's hand touched the crystal doorknob, Karim whispered something to Yasmine, who hushed him with a guilty glance at Ellie.

Her suspicion rising, Ellie turned back to ask direct questions. Even as she opened her mouth, a disturbing sound reached her ears. "Wait! Do you hear that?"

"What?" the children all asked.

Ellie put a finger to her lips and heard it again—the unmistakable squeak of a cinder sprite in distress. The mother sprite heard it too and answered with sharp whistles.

"Where is it coming from? Is there another baby sprite in the suite?" Ellie snatched an empty cage and the spray bottle from her pack then stepped slowly along the passage with her head tilted to better judge direction. "How many sprites did you catch?"

The older children shrugged. "There were a whole bunch of them," Karim said, trying to be helpful.

Ellie pinpointed the sound: It came from behind a closed door on her left. Even as she paused to make certain, there came one last plaintive squeal followed by the distinctive *whoomp* of a sprite going ember. She flung open the door and rushed into a chamber so dark that she immediately spotted the orange glow of the baby sprite, which took one look at her and ran, igniting a swath of dangling fabric as it disappeared beneath a large piece of furniture.

With one flying leap, Ellie caught up the cloth and beat out the flame with her gloved hands, then sprawled on the floor and shoved herself under what seemed to be a bed. In the pulsing glow of the sprite she saw a stray sock and a pair of men's bedroom slippers. The baby sprite cowered against the wall, well out of her reach, igniting unlucky dust bunnies with bright little flares.

Ellie scooted toward it using her elbows, shoving the cage and spray bottle ahead of her, kicking and wriggling to force certain portions of her anatomy into the tight space, and losing both shoes in the process. "It's okay, little one," she assured the sprite breathlessly while moving her bottle into position. It hissed and crackled in reply. Once ignited, sprites were not so cute. Their big eyes glowed red, and their furry bodies looked like coals in a bonfire.

A quick spray, a softer hiss, and the tiny sprite dissolved into a puddle. "Rafiq," she said, "would you bring me my pack, please?"

"Sure, Ellie," he said. Ellie thought she heard giggles from the children. Only then did she realize how unladylike was her position despite the once-piece coverall she wore while working.

"Do my feet look funny, sticking out from under the bed?" she asked, then sneezed, smacking her chin on the floor below and rebounding her head into the bed frame above. "Oh, ouch!" she moaned. "It's dusty under here!"

The giggles became much louder, and Ellie distinctly heard and felt something move on the bed above her. Were the children bouncing up there? Springs squeaked, and feet thumped on the floor. She heard whispers and more laughter. "Rafiq, did you find my pack? Can you please slide my scoop to me?"

"Here it is," the boy said, easily scooting under the bed alongside her. She took the pack and awkwardly felt around in it for her scoop. "Where's the sprite?" Rafiq asked, peering around in the shadows.

The room suddenly got much brighter; someone had pushed open the draperies.

"Right here." Ellie carefully scooped up a limp, gooey lump that bore no resemblance to the lively creature it had been only moments before.

"Eew, yuck," the boy said, and quickly backed away. "It stinks worse than the others did."

"Sulfur," Ellie told him. "This spray isn't very effective against the smell. Now can you look in the sack and find my other spray bottle, please? It fixes things."

More whispering and giggles above, and again the bed springs creaked. What were those kids doing up there?

She reached back her hand, and Rafiq laid the bottle in her palm then scooted out from under the bed, complaining loudly about the stink. Thinking of her favorite flower, Ellie sprayed the sticky place on the floor where the sprite had been, and the smell transformed into a faint scent of carnations while the stain disappeared. Now to back out of this very tight place, bringing along the cage and two bottles. She squirmed and shimmied carefully backward, shoving and pulling her tools across the floor. It was quiet in the room. Had the children run off?

But after her kicking legs had emerged and she had to work harder to fit her hips under the bed frame, the giggles started all over again. She suddenly felt hot enough to "go ember" like a sprite herself. "Yes, I know, I'm too big to fit. But I did it, you must admit." She squeezed the top half of herself into open air then rolled over and sat up, blinking in a ray of direct sunlight. Seeing Rita's feet dangling off the bed beside her, she pulled off her gloves, reached out and caught one little shoe to make the child giggle, then froze.

And slowly turned her head.

Only inches away, a pair of big, dark eyes gazed at her from the edge of the bed. He lay flat on his belly with his stubbled chin resting on his brown hands. Glossy black hair stood out at all angles from his head.

"Good morning, Miss Ellie," said Prince Omar

with a smile. "I hear you've just rescued me from a fiery death."

CHAPTER TWO

WHEN OMAR AWOKE TO FIND YOUNGER SIBLINGS crawling over and around him, his first reaction was to shout—but a hand covered his mouth before a sound emerged. "Ellie the magic-creature lady is under your bed," whispered Yasmine. "Please don't scare her away."

Ellie? I must be dreaming, he thought. But the stink of sulfur and the sound of Ellie's muffled voice snuffed that idea. He pulled his sister's hand away and whispered the obvious question: "Why is she under my bed?"

"She's catching a cinder sprite that lit your

sheets on fire."

Ellie Calmer is under my bed, he thought. No, it couldn't be. But when he heard Ellie speak again then sneeze, and something bumped the bed from beneath, he threw off the blanket and sat upright, blood racing through his veins, while his little siblings snorted and giggled.

"What?" he hissed, running one hand over his hair. Then panic struck. He wore only a pair of pajama pants covered in smiling green sea monsters, a gag gift from his sister Layla. Carefully he climbed out of bed and tiptoed across to where his white robe hung on a hook. While he tied its belt around his waist, Rafiq hissed to draw his attention, pointed at a pair of bare feet sticking out from beneath the hanging coverlet, then pointed at Omar and pantomimed laughing.

Even he knew about Omar's hopeless crush. Great.

Ellie asked Rafiq if he was coming, and the little terror slithered under the bed, taking with him the pack Omar recognized as Ellie's. Sunlight struck Omar's face, making him wince—Yasmine was pushing open the heavy drapes. It was broad daylight. How late had he slept? His clothes were scattered across the room, and his travel bag lay open near the foot of the bed. He snatched up a sock and his jeans, then dropped them in a heap. What a disaster zone! He was a mess.

He couldn't just stand here in his robe and watch Ellie scoot out from under his bed. Should he pretend to be asleep? She would never believe it. He hurried to climb back on the bed. Rita and Karim bounced up to join him again, giggling like little maniacs.

He heard Ellie and Rafiq talking, then his rascal brother emerged from hiding, wearing a mocking grin. Something sprayed, and a lovely scent replaced the sulphur stink. Omar heard Ellie shuffling. He looked down at himself and tugged the robe to cover his bare chest. No matter what he did or said, this would be embarrassing for her. There was no getting around that.

Maybe if he looked relaxed and okay with it, as if girls emerged from under his bed every morn—No, wait, not that! How about if he looked grateful that she'd come to rescue him . . . which he was. He carefully lay down flat on the bed with his face at the edge . . . and immediately knew he'd done the wrong thing. But pretty much anything he did would be the wrong thing. At this point, he could only try to make her feel as comfortable as possible. If that were possible.

His heart pounded in his chest, and his mouth went dry as he watched her decidedly feminine figure emerge feet-first from beneath his bed. Things like this simply didn't happen to him—a beautiful girl under his bed, the very girl he had wished for years to know but was always too shy to approach. He wasn't altogether certain yet that he wasn't dreaming, particularly when Ellie turned her tousled head and looked directly into his eyes.

Instead of stammering as he'd expected, he spoke with apparent confidence. Maybe her disheveled state and evident embarrassment served to level the playing field? Her horrified expression worried him. What was she thinking? Did he look that bad? His heart pounded like a drum in his chest, but the need to set her at ease gave him a voice. "It's remarkable how you can revive cinder sprites."

She released a little gasp. "I am so sorry! I didn't know you were in here," she said, her voice tremulous, her cheeks bright pink and smudged with dust. "I had no idea!" She shoved shoes onto her bare feet, shoes made of clear glass like the sprite cage beside her on the floor. Her feet and ankles were very pretty. So was the rest of her.

"I arrived during the night," he explained. The sunlight falling through the window turned Ellie's hair to silvery gold. Gazing at her, Omar felt almost poetic, a strange sensation for a mathematician. Sadly, nothing poetic came out of his mouth. Rita climbed onto his back and tugged at his hair, which was distracting, not to mention painful, but he maintained focus. "Next thing I knew, I had kids bouncing on my back." He propped up on his elbows and reached one hand to loosen Rita's grasp on his hair. "So, how did a cinder sprite get in here?"

Ellie opened her mouth, but Rafiq spoke first. "It was Karim's idea. After breakfast we found the mother and her babies running around in the garden."

"There was nobody else around," Karim added, "and they looked scared."

"We put them in a bucket and brought them inside to take care of them," Yasmine contributed.

"They were so sweet! We didn't know they would catch fire."

"There was more than one in the suite?" Omar asked, looking to Ellie for confirmation. Her mouth still hung open, and her eyes were wide. His plan to soothe her fears didn't seem to be working.

She stopped gaping at him long enough to answer: "Yes, but only one in here. It must have squeezed under the door. I was preparing to leave when I heard it squeak and ignite."

"Oof!" he grunted. Rita had flopped down hard on his back, driving the air from his lungs. Enough of that. He quickly sat upright and crossed his legs, dragging his baby sister around to perch on one knee. She protested, then squirmed away and stood behind him, wrapping her little arms around his neck and shoving him forward. While doubled over, he got a close look at his sea-monster-covered pajama legs and died a little inside. If asked at that moment, Omar might have traded away one or two younger siblings for a monkey.

"The sprites ran all over the sitting room," Karim was saying. "They squeaked like this—" He performed an excellent imitation. "And they went 'poof' and Ellie had to spray 'em before the whole castle burnt down. You missed seeing all the fun."

"Oh, not all of it," he said, then realized how that might be interpreted and nearly choked. The pink in Ellie's cheeks spread over her entire face as she stuffed her gloves into her pack. Had he blown it completely? Her hands trembled, but she didn't seem angry or disgusted. Hope revived.

Karim scampered from the room, practicing his sprite calls.

"My baby one burnded up." Tugging at his robe, Rita spoke directly into Omar's ear, her lips wet and tickling. He cringed. "But Ellie says he's all right. She scoopded him up and put him in a box."

"And just now she scooped up the one from under your bed," Rafiq said. "It was all gooey and stinky."

Yasmine spoke quietly from her perch on a chair near the door, her eyes wide and serious. "If Ellie hadn't come in and put out the fire it made, you might have died."

"But all is well now, and I will send the sprites away to a safe place where they won't harm anyone," Ellie said, mostly to the children. Her soothing voice flowed over Omar's spirit like warm honey. Then she looked up at him, all business again, with a worried crease between her brows. "I haven't seen their nanny all morning."

He shrugged. "I would have said Rafiq was old enough to watch the little ones, but it seems I would have been wrong."

Rafiq glowered. "I didn't know sprites were dangerous," he mumbled.

"Though you have been told many times every summer not to approach wild animals, particularly not magical creatures." Omar spoke without removing his gaze from Ellie's pale face while she scooted over to spray the burned sheet with a bottle of magical liquid. As the linen fabric mended itself, a fragrance reminiscent of a summer evening beside the lake replaced the scorched scent. Ellie looked up, caught his gaze, and blushed again. Quickly she turned back to her pack.

Rafiq scrambled to his feet and left the room in a huff, mumbling under his breath.

"Miss Ellie," Omar said, hoping she might look at him again, "I apologize for causing you extra trouble. I shouldn't have slept in so late. Usually Asmaa, the nanny, can keep this little mob under control, but obviously she needed help this morning."

Her gaze flashed up to meet his. "I don't blame you. But whatever will your parents say about . . . about this?" She waved one hand vaguely, but he knew what she meant.

"You saved the day," he said firmly, "and that is all we will tell them."

He held her gaze for a golden moment, but then her lips set in a firm line and she focused on stuffing her spray bottles into her pack. She was not her usual confident, competent self. His hope slipped again. Did she like him at all, or was he upsetting her?

Yasmine abruptly rushed from the room. He caught a glimpse of his little sister's expression and wondered what had upset her.

"Yasmine, wait!" Rita shouted in his ear, then lost her balance and nearly pulled Omar over by the neck of his robe in her hurry to follow her sister. He quickly grabbed her arms and helped her slide safely off the bed. She landed on her backside anyway, then rolled over, pushed herself up, and ran into the hallway, shouting "My sprite! My sprite!" in a squeaky voice.

Aware that the dream was about to end, Omar slid off the bed and adjusted his robe just as Ellie scrambled to her feet. She looked up, stammered "Th-thank you," and fled, her glass shoes clopping on the hardwood floor.

Omar snatched up her forgotten pack and followed close behind, his bare feet padding silently. "Thank you again for saving us all," he said, aware that he sounded foolish but unable to stop himself. "Miss Ellie, please . . ."

She took the pack from him with lowered eyes and mumbled thanks, slung it over her shoulder, then paused inside the suite's entry door to stack glass boxes in her arms. Now that sprites filled them, they no longer fit into her pack.

"If you'll wait a moment while I change, I can help you carry them down," Omar said. Any excuse for more time with her.

"Oh, don't bother," she said shortly. "I've carried more cages than this before."

"It's no bother at all," he began, just as the lock rattled and the door swung open to reveal the children's nanny, her gray hair in a tangle, her expression both angry and worried.

"Where are the children?" she asked.

"Uh, around here somewhere. What happened to you, Asmaa?"

"That young viper locked me into a garden shed!" she snapped. "Lured me in there with some story about a puppy, then shut and barred the door. If one of the gardeners hadn't come along, I'd be there yet." Then her face softened. "Welcome, Prince Omar. I'm glad you've joined us."

"Thank you, Asmaa. I apologize for my siblings' behavior."

"It was Rafiq, of course," she growled. Then her gaze moved to study Ellie in her dusty coverall. "Do I know this person?"

He cringed inwardly at her disapproving tone. "This is Miss Ellie Calmer. The children brought cinder sprites into the suite, and the castle might be burning right now if Miss Calmer had not rushed to our rescue."

"Indeed." Asmaa's dark eyes narrowed. "And you not yet dressed, Omar."

His face burned. "I didn't arrive until nearly three in the morning."

While they were speaking, Ellie slipped around the door and into the main hall, the cages stacked in her arms. Omar took a few steps toward his room. "Asmaa, the kids are around here somewhere. I've got to get dressed and help Miss Ellie with those cages."

With any luck, he thought, he might catch Ellie on the stairs. With any luck, she would find the load too unwieldy and need to stop once or twice. In his room he threw on shorts, t-shirt, and shoes, then dashed after her, guessing she would use the service stairs. She was halfway down the second flight, precariously balancing her load of squeaking sprites, when he caught up and passed her.

"Here, let me take some of those," he offered, and she gave such a start that he seized the top cage to save it from bouncing down the remaining stairs.

"No, no, please!" Even as he took another cage from her load, she gave him an imploring look. "I could lose my position here if you're seen helping me or even talking with me. And if the director heard that I was in your . . . your bedroom . . ." She visibly shuddered.

His hope withered. "I won't tell anyone, and I'll make certain the children keep quiet. They definitely don't want you to leave Faraway Castle," he said. "I won't try to help if it'll cause you trouble. That's the last thing I want."

She moved on down the last few stairs. At the base of that flight, he replaced the two cages atop her load. "I'm really sorry if I . . . if I upset you, Miss Ellie. I wouldn't hurt you for anything." He gave her an awkward little bow.

She looked up, and he saw something in her gaze that was nothing like anger or disgust. The corners of her lips turned up slightly. But then her lashes lowered, and she continued down the next flight of stairs. He headed back upstairs toward the suite, his heart heavy.

His parents wanted him to choose a wife this summer from among the princesses and ladies who visited the resort every year. He had delayed joining his family for as long as possible, dreading the ordeal he knew lay ahead, but now he was glad he'd come.

Not that the king and queen of Khenifra would accept Ellie Calmer as a prospective wife for their son, but at least he would be near her for the next few weeks. He might glimpse her in the halls or at the lake or anywhere on the grounds, and perhaps he would find, or invent, a respectable opportunity to speak with her again.

He was a prince. Ellie was a member of the staff, a working girl. Finding a harmless and acceptable way to interact with her would be no easy task.

What good was an expensive education and a supposedly clever brain if he couldn't think of a solution to this equation?

CHAPTER THREE

I N HER CONFUSION, ELLIE TOOK A WRONG TURN AND left the castle through the main lobby, a path she usually avoided to keep from encountering guests. To her dismay, as she pushed open a glass door with her hip and maneuvered the stack of cages through the opening, two girls in short sundresses and strappy sandals approached on the front walkway and could not miss seeing her.

The Honorable Gillian Montmorency and Lady Raquel Cambout, both from the nation of Auvers and near Ellie's age, were two of her least favorites among the hundreds of yearly visitors at Faraway Castle. Like most of the guests, they had never bothered to learn her name and always spoke to her as if she were a dim-witted child or scullery maid.

Their conversation broke off as soon as they saw her. Gillian, a stunning beauty with red-gold hair, asked sharply, "What are you carrying? I hear squeaking."

"Cinder sprites," Ellie said, peering around her stack of cages.

The girl's lip curled. "How did you get so disgustingly dirty?"

"Capturing cinder sprites." Ellie schooled her face into a pleasant expression. She hoped.

"I've never seen one." Raquel, a slender brunette, peered into a cage, her nose wrinkled. "All I can see is straw. You caught them inside the castle? Where?"

"The Zeidan children found them outside and sneaked them into the royal suite."

The girls looked at each other and sputtered with laughter. "Those adorable rascals," Gillian said in a syrupy tone. "Good thing we have pest control available." Her mocking gaze swept Ellie from head to toe.

"I don't suppose you could tell us if the rumor

about Prince Omar is true," Raquel said, her vivid blue eyes eager.

"What rumor is that, my lady?" Ellie inquired, striving to sound pleasant. One of her arms began to cramp up, so she shifted the cages in her grasp.

Sensing her distress, one of the sprites whistled, and a chorus of squeals followed. "It's all right, babies," Ellie said, trying to calm herself as well as the little creatures. "I'll get you home soon."

"Can't you keep those beasts quiet while we talk?" Raquel complained. "We heard that Prince Omar arrived during the night. Did you see him?"

Ellie paused, but there was no avoiding such a direct question. "I did."

The girls gave little shrieks, giddy with excitement, and began to formulate plans to claim his time and attention. They were still talking when Ellie walked away, unwilling to hear more.

No matter how she tried to view Prince Omar as just another resort guest, even the thought of his marrying one of those two harpies made her want to throw something, hard. Preferably at their heads. Or maybe a kick in the shin would be more satisfying.

The cages in her arms seemed heavier by the moment, yet she walked quickly along the path leading to the staff cabins. "If I don't stop thinking about—" cutting off sharply, she glanced around, saw no one near, then continued in a half-whisper "—Omar, I'll either get myself fired or go stark, raving crazy."

The mother sprite muttered irritably.

"I'm sorry," Ellie sighed. "I'm upsetting you. It's okay, little sprites, my angst isn't about you. You're going to be fine. I've got to stop thinking about . . . him."

Omar wasn't the crown prince. With two older brothers, he was third in line for the throne— primogeniture in Khenifra being through the male line—but he was still considered a hot marital catch. Probably because he was the handsomest of the older three brothers and wealthy in his own right.

"Girls like Gillian and Raquel can't begin to appreciate his best qualities," Ellie told the sprites. "He doesn't think of himself as anything special. This morning he almost seemed worried about offending me." After a pause, she huffed a laugh. She must have imagined the puppy-dog hopefulness in his eyes.

"Almost there now," she said, striving to keep a cheery tone.

Ellie's cottage was set amid other staff lodgings, comfortable one-bedroom homes offering no view but decent privacy. All were of weathered stone with crisp white trim, green shutters, and a red door. She released the magical lock with a verbal request, and the door swung open before her. A chorus of whistles and one shrill shout greeted her from the cages of captured creatures lining one corner of her tiny living room. "Yes, I'm back and will feed you all shortly. Have a little patience please. I brought new friends."

With a relieved sigh, she lowered her fresh stack of cages to the floor. "Whew!" She was a strong girl, but so many cages at once had made an unwieldy load. She'd almost dropped one on the stairs—the memory now made her cringe.

"Should I have let Omar help me carry them?" The thought escaped in a whisper. Briefly she imagined walking across the resort beside him, their arms full of cages, chatting easily about cinder sprites and . . . whatever princes talk about. Maybe he would have come in and stayed for a cup of tea.

The mind picture of him standing in her little cottage made her heart do crazy things. "My imagination will be the death of me," she sighed.

The resident sprites now exchanged gentle squeaks of greeting with the newcomers, but the imp, a tiny green humanoid who'd been caught destroying cabbages in the kitchen garden, continued to berate Ellie in its shrill voice and unknown language. The glass cage insulated all forms of magic, so its curses were harmless. She gave it a smile, then opened the first cage and gently lifted out a solid-black baby sprite, the one from Omar's bedroom.

He was still groggy, blinking his big eyes and twitching his ears. His little clawed feet tickled her hand. "You are simply the cutest thing ever," Ellie murmured, then opened the mother's cage and set the baby down beside her. Making comforting little chirps, the mother sprite checked him over with her busy tongue.

One by one Ellie moved the other four, and the mother's cage grew to accommodate them all. Ellie cleaned out the empty cages, filled them with fresh hay, then gently squeezed them back into one-inch cubes before returning them to her pack. "I hope I never need that many at once again, but it's best to be prepared." She added several more to the pack, just in case. They were almost weightless at this size, after all.

Finished, she sat back on her heels and heaved a deep sigh. Focusing on the sprites, she spoke in her most encouraging tone. "You'll all be happy at the Gamekeeper's sprite refuge. Plenty to eat always, safe places to raise a family, and good company."

Next she served carrots, kale, and endive to her furry guests—fresh greens helped to quench their fiery spirits. The gardeners kept her supplied with beetle larvae for the imp, which crouched over its food and stuffed its mouth, still muttering between bites. The sprites tucked in, puffing softly.

Her living room was feeling crowded with a dozen cages stacked against the wall. It would soon be time to send for the Gamekeeper to collect her little captives. The other sprites had been quite patient about their wait, content to gossip among themselves and eat good food, but they would all welcome open spaces and freedom.

Ellie poured tea to brew then flopped into a chair and tipped her head back. She was missing the noon meal at the castle, but she wasn't hungry, just thirsty. And emotionally drained.

A picture popped into her head of Prince Omar seated cross-legged on his bed with Rita's little arms around his neck, his hair standing on end, and shy excitement in his beautiful dark eyes. She didn't mean to remember his pajama pants and white bathrobe, let alone the smooth brown skin of his neck and chest, but every detail seemed imprinted on her mind.

Shaking her head to banish the image, she leaped to her feet and rushed into her bedroom, where she stared into the small mirror hanging over her chest of drawers . . . and groaned. Soot and dust streaked her cheeks and chin. Her blonde hair was straggly and looked grayish and faded, like ashes. Even her eyes were gray. Her coverall, though neatly fitted to her figure, was smudged and dusty and made her look like a tall, skinny boy. She was colorless and dirty and couldn't begin to compete with the glamour of Raquel or Gillian, one a sultry brunette, the other a golden-haired china doll.

"I sat there like a lump on his floor," she whispered at her reflection, "and stared at him. So rude! But he tried to talk with me. He really tried! And then he hurried to catch up with me on the stairs." Yet she would be a fool to imagine that he genuinely returned her interest.

While she showered and combed out her hair, Ellie thought back to her first real interaction with Omar three years ago, the night of a wedding celebration for some important people whose names she had long since forgotten. Ellie was assigned to serve drinks to the guests and keep their glasses filled. The meal had ended without mishap, but later, while Ellie walked among the tables with an overfilled pitcher of lemonade, she had noticed that Omar's glass was empty.

He and his older brother Taim were talking with great animation as she stood behind his chair—she'd caught such phrases as "interquartile range" and "permutation formula" and realized she didn't speak his language, which saddened her. While he was distracted, the princess seated beside Omar held up his glass, and Ellie started to fill it. Not until she finished pouring and the princess moved the glass away did either of them notice the spreading dark patch on Omar's suit jacket. Lemonade had dribbled down the side of the pitcher onto his back.

While Omar talked on unaware, gesturing with both hands, Ellie took a towel from its loop at her waist, started to reach for the wet spot, then reconsidered. "Your Highness?" she said, but it came out as a whisper.

Taim gave her a quizzical look and interrupted Omar's mathematical discourse. "This young person desires your attention."

Ellie could still picture Omar's long, thick lashes lifting as he turned to regard her with some surprise. His expression softened into a shy smile, striking her dumb. He opened his mouth, but nothing came out. He closed it, swallowed, and tried again. "Is something wrong, Miss . . . ? Er, I'm afraid I don't know your name."

"E-Ellie," she stuttered. "And I spilled lemonade down your back. Don't you feel it?"

His eyes went wide. At eighteen he had looked more boyish, but those eyes had been just as devastating. "Uh, yes, I guess I do feel rather damp." He asked for her towel, and she watched helplessly as he reached over his shoulder and tried to soak up the sticky juice. The princess took the towel from him and rubbed at the places he couldn't reach, talking all the while about the stupid, clumsy girl who had ruined his fine dress coat. But Omar frowned, took the towel back, and stood up in that narrow space. "Here." His voice cracked, and he cleared his throat, holding out the towel. "I think I . . . I mean . . . Thank you, Miss Ellie."

Then he had stood there looking down at her.

And she had stood there looking up at him.

Remembering this, Ellie smiled and shook her head. Now she realized how bashful and embarrassed he had been. And how completely he had ignored that princess and his brother.

During the six years since she first laid eyes on him, Ellie had told herself countless times not to be a fool—Omar was a prince. But every year when his family arrived at the resort in late June, she had sighed and dreamed of him. Many times he had smiled shyly at her and sent her heart and head spinning—but today marked the first time she had spoken with him since the lemonade incident.

Her position as magical-wildlife controller had

finally brought her into his charmed circle but was unlikely to do so twice. In years to come she would cringe over the memory of *thanking* him . . . for what? For being incredibly hot and allowing her to stare at him? What must he have thought? Her face burned all over again. She looked at herself in the bathroom mirror and watched the blush spread.

"Enough obsessing over the unattainable," she said firmly, pointing the comb at her reflection. A pink face was no better than a pale one, but at least her hair no longer looked ashen. "Time for work."

She checked on the new sprites before heading outside. The babies, fully recovered, now snuggled up to their sweet little mother. "It wasn't your fault you were inside the castle," Ellie assured her. "You can return to the garden if you like."

Sensing only uncertainty from the tired little sprite, she spoke a soothing farewell. "Everybody relax, and I'll see you later!"

Ellie spent the misty afternoon helping her friend Rosa, Faraway Castle's head gardener, catch another imp in the kitchen garden. She first talked the magical trap into appearing harmless and cozy like a pile of compost—an imps' favorite nest—then, at Rosa's suggestion, she baited it with baby lettuces.

"Imps usually eat insect larvae, so I rarely disturb them, but lately they've taken to devouring my greens," Rosa explained. "I could probably eliminate them myself, but your live-trap methods are kinder."

While Ellie finished setting the trap, she pondered Rosa's possible methods for eradicating imps. Might she set her tiger lilies on their trail? A frightful thought! Rosa, only seventeen, had advanced to the position of head gardener for good reason. Chuck and Tasha, a pair of dwarfs who'd worked in the garden since before Ellie first came to Faraway Castle, occasionally dropped hints about their young supervisor, implying that she had more ability with plants than anyone else suspected and praising her to the skies.

"Why so mopey today?" Rosa's voice interrupted Ellie's thoughts as they exited the kitchen garden and descended a trellis-covered stairway into a lush topiary collection. Rosa brushed her hand over the leafy wing of a topiary heron.

Ellie blinked. Had she really seen the heron bob its head? No, it was just a beautifully trimmed boxwood shrub.

Rosa gave her a sly glance. "My guess is boy trouble."

Ellie smiled. "I don't spend enough time with boys to have any trouble. What boy would I want?"

Rosa's lips curled into a wise smile. "One you cannot have, of course."

"You know too much," Ellie retorted in a teasing tone, "which is dangerous—especially for someone as mysterious as you are. Jeralee and I ought to spy on you again in retaliation."

"I wish you wouldn't," Rosa said quickly, and her glance held . . . fear? Regret?

"No worries," Ellie assured her with a rush of guilt. "I haven't the time to be nosy these days."

Why was Rosa so secretive? She had brilliant skill with plants and worked longer hours than the rest of the staff. She was sweet, occasionally witty, and quiet. Other than her Evoran accent, she offered no clues about her past, and she always dressed in unflattering work clothes and wore her hair in a long braid down her back. Since the day she first arrived at Faraway Castle two years ago, the girl hadn't left the grounds for longer than an hour or two.

She was a mystery.

At present, however, Ellie didn't have a brain cell free for wondering about Rosa's secrets. Her own life was complicated enough.

"Since I'm here, I might as well make myself useful. Where shall I work this afternoon?" she asked.

The girls were trimming shrubbery when Ellie sensed her trap snapping shut. A high-pitched scream rolled down the hillside from the kitchen garden. "Caught it!" She dropped her shears and started off at a run, with Rosa close behind.

The imp stamped around inside the cage, shaking its fists and undoubtedly swearing in its high-decibel language. "You're a girl, aren't you?" Ellie commented as she gently tipped the furious creature into one of her glass cages. "I wonder if I don't have your mate locked up in my room."

That task finished, she straightened up and stretched her aching back.

"Thank you so much," Rosa said, "for the garden work as well as for trapping that little lettuce-ravager."

"You're welcome. You know I enjoy it." Ellie was just knocking garden dirt from her glass clogs when her wristband emitted its magical alert. "What now?"

A quick glance informed her. "No emergency. I think it's from the director's office."

Rosa raised a quizzical brow. "Hmm. Wonder what that could be about."

Something in her tone alerted Ellie. "What do you mean?"

"Just before you got here, Jeralee told me about cinder sprites in the royal suite." Rosa's tone expressed both concern and amusement. "Gossip spreads like strangleweed."

"Great. Just great." Ellie's shoulders drooped. "I was only doing my job. Gotta go! Have to drop this imp off at my cottage before I report in." With that, she made her escape.

Who leaked that story? And why must everyone at Faraway Castle demand to know everyone else's business? Rosa knew about Ellie's crush on Prince Omar. She must know as well as anyone how silly it would be even to imagine a happy ending for a staff member with a royal prince.

Ellie dropped the imp off in her cabin then sprinted to the castle, the cages in her pack clinking at every step. The director of Faraway Castle Resort did not take kindly to waiting, and for three years now she'd been looking for some reason to dismiss Ellie. Madame lacked the authority to directly fire Ellie, but she would be certain to report any infraction to the Gamekeeper.

Madame Genevieve seemed to despise every female member of the castle staff and found any romantic relationship appalling. Speculation was rife about her past. Had the director been spurned by a lover? Left at the altar?

A few of the guys insisted she was the hatchet-murderer type and probably had seven former husbands buried in hidden graves on resort grounds.

Yet when Ellie stood in the director's office, returning the woman's stare, she couldn't help thinking how handsome Madame was. Tall, statuesque, with regular features, good teeth, abundant dark hair, and stunning green eyes. Her expression was the problem: cold, resentful, and forbidding.

Madame Genevieve regarded Ellie over the tops of her spectacles. "I have only moments to deal with you, Miss Calmer, so be truthful. I hold in my hand a note claiming that you removed cinder sprites from the royal guest suite, thereby saving the Zeidan family and possibly the entire castle from incineration, and that you afterward repaired all damage inflicted by the pests. It was written by Prince Omar of Khenifra on behalf of his royal parents and siblings." Madame's strange eyes seemed to peer into Ellie's brain. "Do you deserve such commendation?"

Ellie's spine was ramrod straight, and her gaze remained fixed on the letter. "I did my job, Madame, that's all. This morning Sira the brownie alerted me that the Zeidan children had captured a family of sprites in the gardens and sneaked them into the family suite. I captured all six sprites and confined them in cages, then mended the damage they caused. They are currently in my cabin, pending either release or transfer to the Gamekeeper."

"Indeed," said the director, thoughtfully tapping

the note with one finger. "Have you ever spoken with Prince Omar Zeidan before today?"

"Only once, Madame, and that was several years ago, after I spilled lemonade on his coat at a banquet."

"I see." Madame's eye twitched. "Very well, Miss Calmer. You are aware of our fraternization rules. Carry on." She waved one hand and returned her attention to the papers on her desk.

Thus Ellie was warned.

As if this warning had not annihilated her remaining peace of mind, another blow was yet to fall. That evening, on her way to the cafeteria with a few summer-staff gardeners, she encountered a large group of guests in the corridor outside the banquet hall, including Prince Omar with Raquel and Gillian pasted to his arms. Omar brightened and opened his mouth as if to greet her, but Gillian spoke first: "Well, if it isn't Cinder Ellie!"

Raquel added, "Played in the ashes and soot today, Cinder Ellie?"

As soon as they were past, Ellie politely excused herself to her coworkers and took the service stairs down to the kitchen, where she begged a bowl of soup. With shrill laughter still ringing in her ears, she sat on the floor to eat among the brownies, who welcomed her, and the hobgoblins, who did not.

Geraldo gave her an accusing glare and growled, "Only two crumbs tonight, and neither of them chocolate. Hmph!"

CHAPTER FOUR

THE NEXT MORNING ONE OF THE SUPERVISORS, Bence, a gruff, balding, former drill-sergeant, hailed her outside the cafeteria.

"Calmer, you're assigned lake patrol this week and next."

"Lake patrol?" Her responsibilities as magical-creature controller made lake patrol impractical. "What if I get a call?"

He shrugged. "We'll deal with it. We're short a lifeguard, so get going. You know the drill; things haven't changed much since you last worked."

Ellie nodded and tried to smile. "I'll eat fast."

"Do that." Bence wasn't mean, just focused.

The patrol assignment was great—she loved being on the lake. But its suddenness was suspicious. Prince Omar never played in the lake. Rugby, polo, cross-country riding, tennis, football, archery, fencing—he enjoyed all these and more. He even swam laps in the indoor pool. But outdoor water sports? Never. Which was odd, since when Ellie first came to work at the camp, Omar had been a talented water-skier and wakeboarder, a daredevil off the ski-ramp. She had her suspicions about why he avoided the lake, but no proof.

Instead of breakfasting with her friends, she snatched a few hard-boiled eggs and a banana in the kitchen and ate quickly. Sira tapped on her knee. "This morning a coffee cake rose unevenly, so we gave it to Geraldo, and now all the hobgoblins are fighting over it out on the back porch."

Ellie chuckled. "Then they're happy. Since I'm on lake duty I won't be around the castle much this week, but I'll be praying for showers of cake crumbs."

Brownies look mournful even when blissfully happy, but now Sira looked deeply concerned as

well. Ellie quickly amended: "I mean, I hope
Geraldo behaves himself. I don't really want it to
rain cake . . . Never mind."

Sira blinked her melancholy eyes and said,
"Yes, Miss Ellie." And Ellie headed back to her
cottage to change into swim gear, berating herself.
Why did she so often forget that brownies take
everything literally? Poor little Sira!

All that day she patrolled the sparkling
mountain lake on her scooter, enjoying the
beauty, keeping watch for the lake monster, and
handing out a few warnings. After her quick lunch
break, she picked up a water-skier who refused to
climb back into the ski boat.

Ellie recognized this unfortunate little skier, a
princess from Nsukka, as a friend of Rafiq and
Yasmine. Three other children in the boat,
probably her brothers, shouted orders and
suggestions at the girl in the water, who kept
trying to swim away.

The boat's driver, who also shared the young
girl's black skin and nearly perfect features, must
be an older sister. She too shouted at the
swimmer, not unkindly, but frustration laced her
voice.

Ellie sensed the little princess's embarrassment, exhaustion, and reluctance to rejoin her companions after repeated failures to remain upright on her skis for more than a few seconds. She moved her scooter in close. "Would you like to ride back to shore with me?" she asked, infusing her voice with optimism.

The girl nodded and stopped paddling. "Yes, please," she said, her eyes imploring.

After hauling the exhausted princess up behind her on the scooter, Ellie shouted to the others in the boat, "Don't worry, I'll take her safely back to shore."

"Thanks!" called the sister, then maneuvered the boat around to pick up the abandoned skis. Moments later, the ski boat roared off.

Ellie felt the child's shuddering sobs at her back. Over the past few years she had learned that words didn't matter as much as her tone when it came to rebuilding confidence, even in a human. "So now it's just you and me and the fish," she said. "What is your name, Your Highness?"

"Aisosa."

"I am pleased to meet you, Princess Aisosa.

How old are you?"

"I will be twelve in October."

"I was twelve when I first came here to work. Don't let anyone fool you—it takes time and practice to develop balance and strength enough to ski well, and none of those kids learned in a day."

"My sister stood up on her first try," Aisosa grumbled.

"Well, good for her. I sure didn't! It took me two summers of practice before I could stay up for more than a minute. Anyway, I bet you're good at other sports. You look like a runner."

She felt the girl nod against her life jacket. "I do like to run fast," she said. "I like the lake best from inside a boat."

Ellie grinned. "I hope you like my scooter too. It's pretty fun. Want to see what it can do?"

"We won't tip over?"

"Nope. I'll be careful. Hold on to my waist and nod when you're ready, okay?"

As soon as Aisosa nodded, Ellie gunned her scooter. "Let's go!" She took the girl for a gentle ride, performing a few loops and figure eights, all the while charming her passenger back into happiness. She was forbidden to use magic on guests, but no matter how she struggled to control it, traces of enchantment frequently slipped into her voice.

As they skimmed past the island, an exotic paradise set in the middle of the mountain lake, Aisosa asked, "Is it true that sirens live there?"

Ellie grinned. She could see two mermaids perched on a flat rock, one combing her long red hair, the other arranging her iridescent tail, but she didn't say so. Sirens remained invisible to unmagical humans unless they deliberately spoke to one, and they called only men. "Yes, they are the reason men and boys are not allowed to drive boats at this end of the lake, and we discourage men from boating at all," she explained over her shoulder. "Guests frequently ignore the warnings, however. Guys hear the rumors and just have to try their luck."

"What do the sirens do?" The girl sounded skeptical.

"When a siren sings to a young man, he believes her voice the most beautiful sound he has ever heard and will do anything to go to her. Sometimes the siren will let him see her, which makes him even more obsessed with her beauty. And then she sends a wave or whirlpool to wreck his boat, leaves him in the water, and laughs."

"That's terrible! Do sirens ever hurt the boys here?" Aisosa asked.

"None of our guests have drowned or even been injured. The sirens aren't allowed to touch them. And there's a bright side: We get several new boats every summer!"

"Why doesn't the resort director send them away?" Aisosa asked. "They don't sound at all nice."

"I agree with you, but many regular guests to Faraway Castle insist that the sirens remain. Want to know a secret? Their singing gives me a headache."

"I thought only men could hear them," Aisosa said.

"I have a little bit of magic, so sometimes I can hear them too. But to me they sound like buzzing hornets."

The little princess laughed. By the time Ellie dropped Aisosa off at the docks, they were fast friends. "I feel happier now," the girl told her as she climbed off the scooter. "I think I'll keep trying to water ski, even if I don't like it much. Rafiq likes to ski."

"His brother Omar used to be amazing on skis and wakeboard," Ellie said without thinking. She hastily added, "Taim and Layla are great skiers too."

Oh dear. She sounded as if she knew the family personally.

"You're awfully nice." Aisosa had a dazzling smile.

"Thank you," Ellie said with genuine warmth. "I think you're pretty awesome too. See you later!"

As she headed back out on patrol, Ellie kicked herself for the slip. For all her magical gift of speech, she had the most trouble keeping control of ordinary words.

⁓◌⌒

On her second day of lake duty, Ellie saw the Zeidan children, along with Aisosa and two of her younger siblings, playing in the water at the beach, which was roped off as a safe area. Ellie scanned the shore eagerly but saw only the nanny seated under a tree with Rita. No sign of the Zeidan parents.

Or of Omar.

She was disappointed. But, she acknowledged to herself, Omar's absence made it easier to concentrate on her work. She needed to get all these silly thoughts about him out of her head anyway.

Around midmorning, while skimming along the north shore of the island, Ellie saw a scaly *something* floating on the surface. Curious, she slowed down to move closer. It was long and thin, much longer than she'd first guessed. Much, much longer. And were those . . . spikes? The lake serpent! It must be sunning itself.

Just as she decided to back off and sneak away, the creature suddenly sank beneath the surface, and her scooter spun helplessly about on the waves.

Heart pounding in her throat, she resumed her patrol, but her thoughts were scrambled. The serpent had never harmed anyone, so far as she knew, but once she had seen it threaten a guest—Omar, actually—and that memory lingered, sometimes in her nightmares.

After that alarming event, the morning was uneventful. Sometime after her lunch break, she was trolling along the northeast shore when screams and shouts reached her ears. They seemed to come from within a small bay, so Ellie gunned her engine and followed the noise.

Among some reeds near the shore, she saw a man in a wetsuit. He appeared to be dragging a small rowboat occupied by three boys, hauling it by its mooring line while they desperately tried to row in the opposite direction. One of the two larger boys stopped rowing to attack him with an oar, but the man caught it and yanked it from his hands. She heard the rumble of the man's voice and saw him snatch something from another boy and throw it onto the nearby bank. The boys were panicked while the man remained eerily calm.

What could she do? She carried no weapons, and that man was big. Her voice was her only weapon. Using it on guests was forbidden . . . but this was an emergency.

As she cautiously approached, the smallest boy, a freckled redhead, called out to her in his treble voice. "Help! Thief! He's stealing our things!"

"It's just a girl," snapped the other redhead, who had to be his older brother. "What could she do to help, idiot?"

Just as Ellie drew breath and opened her mouth, the man said, "Stealing? I took away your fishing poles." He turned to Ellie. "They were fishing."

"We only want catfish and panfish," the biggest boy said, shoving lanky black hair from his face. "We aren't hurting anything."

"You think catfish and panfish don't feel pain?" The man glowered as if the fish were his personal friends. Now she could see that he was young, early twenties at most, with wide shoulders and a rangy build, a short beard, buzz-cut hair, and sunblock on his nose.

Ellie put her scooter into idle and let it drift closer. "The rule is no fishing, with no exceptions," she told the boys, then gave the man a curious look. "Are you new here, sir?"

"I stayed at the resort twice before, most recently six years ago." He kept his focus on the boys.

Six years ago? That would have been her first summer at Faraway Castle. He didn't look familiar.

"What's your name?" she asked.

"Torbjorn. I'm from Hyllestad."

His tone was polite but distant. Guests were often haughty in their manner toward staff members. This guy just seemed distracted.

"I thank you for rescuing the resort's fish," she said. "If you would hand over the boys' fishing gear, I will take it to the office for proper disposal and alert the director to this misconduct." Still seated on her idling scooter, she pulled a pad and pen from a waterproof compartment under her seat then fixed her gaze on the boys. "Names, please."

The boys mumbled their names, spelling them when necessary. She'd been right—the redheads were brothers, and all three were lords' sons from Rathvilly. Then Torbjorn waded out waist-deep and passed their gear to Ellie, who stowed the small tackle box in her storage compartment and laid the fishing poles across her lap.

"Is this everything?" she asked.

The boys nodded.

"What did you use for bait?" the man asked.

"We dug worms in the garden," the youngest boy, Brian, answered warily.

"That was stealing. Put them back where they belong."

Ellie bit her lip to prevent a smile. "He's right," she said. "I'm sure you did not have permission to dig worms."

"The guy is cracked!" Quinn, the big brother, muttered. "Clean off his nut!"

Which may well be true, Ellie mused. On the plus side, the boys didn't dare defy her authority while the big vigilante loomed near. No need to use her magic. She ordered, "Now you boys head directly to the dock and turn in your boat. I must report your offense to Bence, my supervisor."

The dark-haired boy, Desmond, spoke up. "We need our oars back. He took 'em."

As the man waded back to the shore where he'd tossed the oars, Ellie saw something large and gray break the water's surface not far behind him. A fish? She was jumpy after that lake-serpent encounter.

Then, when Torbjorn waded back out to return the oars, the creature appeared again, bumping him in the side. "Back off a minute," she heard him say. To the fish?

Its head appeared at the surface beside him, revealing a wide mouth, small yellow eyes, and trailing whiskers.

"Whoa! I didn't know there were fish that size in this lake," Quinn said.

"That's a monster catfish," said Desmond with awe.

Monster? These kids had no idea what lurked in these waters. A close-up glimpse of the lake serpent might put them off fishing for life!

Once he'd handed over the oars and the coiled mooring line, the man Torbjorn reached out to rub the catfish's broad head. "He's no monster. He's a pet. Years ago, he was hooked by another illegal fisherman"—he pointed to a notch in the fish's broad lip—"but someone rescued him. And he's smart. I haven't been here in six years, yet this fish still remembers me."

"No way!" Desmond said. "I didn't know fish could think."

"And they're protected by law." Torbjorn spoke with calm authority. "From now on, hunt fish with a camera. Maybe you could make friends with one like Fathoms here."

"I'll put the worms back in the garden, mister," Brian piped up.

Torbjorn nodded approval.

Desmond started rowing, and Brian waved to

the fish man. "Goodbye!" he called. "Goodbye, Fathoms." The fish swam after the boat, that big head plowing through the waves, and Brian reached over the side to touch its slimy back. Only Quinn still looked sulky by the time the boat moved out of sight.

Ellie turned to the fish guardian. "I appreciate your assistance, sir."

Standing there in the reedy water, Torbjorn bowed slightly, then for the first time focused on her. "Have there been any siren incidents recently? I mean, do they still live on the island?"

"Why do you ask?" Her guard went up. She backed her scooter, keeping her eyes on him.

"I need to know." The catfish returned and butted against the man's arm. He absently put his arm around its thick body.

"The sirens are still around." She wanted to add "unfortunately" but restrained herself. This guy needed watching, she mused. He was either a genius or a wack job. Maybe both. "Thanks again for the help."

She drove away, leaving Tor among the reeds with his catfish. What a strange dude! At the docks she tied up her scooter, unloaded the tackle box and awkwardly carried three fishing poles toward the lifeguard station. "Whoa," was Bence's comment when she stacked her booty in a corner of the shed.

"Did the boys turn themselves in?" she asked. "I have their names. If they gave me false names, I can identify their faces."

"They did come." He gave her a look. "Did you enchant them?"

"Not a word." Thanks to the fish vigilante.

Bence seemed grudgingly impressed. "Good work."

"Um, there was a man who helped me catch the fishermen. A tall guy in a wetsuit? Said he last stayed at the resort six years ago. His name is Torbjorn from Hyllestad."

Bence's eyes went wide. "No kidding?"

His response was telling. "Who is he, Bence?"

The supervisor looked down and scratched his chin. "Hmm. Well. Sounds like Lord Magnussen."

"Is he a potential problem? Like . . . with the sirens?"

Bence's hand moved to the back of his grizzled neck. "He's an odd one—some kind of scholar, with lots of degrees. Studies magical creatures in the oceans. Naw, I wouldn't worry about him." He gave her a crooked smile.

Feeling somewhat better, Ellie stepped back out on the open dock and heard someone call her name. She turned to see a small herd of Zeidan children scamper across the beach and onto the dock. Their feet pounded along the boards. "Ellie! Cinder Ellie!"

From them, the nickname was no insult. She went down on one knee and opened her arms to receive their exuberant hugs. They were wet, sand-covered, and warm in her arms, and they quite melted her heart. Even Rafiq gave her a quick one-armed hug before backing off with a sheepish face.

"Do you have to be out there on the lake all day?" "Don't you get sunburned?" "Did you really rescue Aisosa?" "Have you seen the lake monster?" "Do you like swimming?" The questions flew at her from all sides, and she could only laugh.

With her arms around Rita and Karim, she said, "I wish I could stay and play with you, but I've got to get back on patrol. But first I will answer your other questions, so listen closely! I apply a charmed spray to protect myself from the sun. I did have the pleasure of meeting your lovely friend Aisosa yesterday. The lake monster was napping this morning just north of the island. And I love swimming. There now." She smiled around at them. "Are you happy?"

Rita's lower lip started to quiver, and Karim said, "But we want *you,* Ellie."

Ellie hugged them close, and when Rita's arms slid around her neck, her heart seemed to expand inside her chest. But she had to set them down and keep them from swarming her again while she said, "Oh, sweeties, maybe we can see each other in the garden or on the beach sometime soon, and then you can tell me about your latest adventures, all right?"

Karim scowled but nodded, and Rita tried to smile, blinking fast. Ellie squeezed Karim's hand, kissed Rita's round cheek, and gave Yasmine and Rafiq loving smiles. "I have to leave now. Will you stand on the beach right over there and wave to me while I drive away?

The children nodded, brightening. Yasmine and Rafiq led their siblings back ashore while Ellie hurried to climb aboard her scooter. She drove out a little way then turned back to face her little fan club. "Soon!" she called.

A little chorus of echoes, smiles, and waves sent her on her way.

CHAPTER FIVE

LLIE AWAKENED ON THE THIRD DAY OF HER lake patrol feeling decidedly blue. She had caught glimpses of Omar only from a distance during the past two days, usually near the guests' dining hall in the company of several other young men, including that odd champion of panfish, Torbjorn. While this was considerably better than seeing him in the company of fawning girls, she wasn't sure whether he noticed her at all.

The Zeidan family always reserved the royal suite for four weeks; Omar had missed the first two weeks, and the third was flying past. Ellie's heart hurt at the thought of not seeing him again for an entire year . . . or ever.

This was bad. This was very bad. Her heartache was nonsensical, of course, for she scarcely knew the boy and had conversed with him only a few times. She was simply infatuated with his looks. And perhaps also with his gentle voice and his reputation as a true gentleman and his mathematical genius and the way he interacted with his younger siblings and . . . She could go on for hours, but what was the point? The brain fever would surely pass once he was out of her life for good.

After feeding the sprites and imps, she slipped into another of her practical swimsuits and a pair of sport shorts—the resort's dress code was stricter for staff than for guests—and pulled her hair into a high ponytail. At least she looked clean, not sooty or gray, she mused while regarding her reflection. The charmed sun-deflecting spray preserved her fair complexion, protected her eyes, and kept her hair from drying out.

She was pretty, she knew, for male guests frequently sought her attention and pelted her with admiring comments on her face and figure, some appreciated, most not so much. But amid crowds of attractive young princesses and noblewomen who frequented beauty spas, wore the latest and most extravagant fashions, and had full access to Prince Omar's time and attention, Ellie felt like a shadow.

Another quick breakfast, a few greetings exchanged with coworkers, and she was off to the lake. The guests usually didn't show up directly after breakfast, so she and three other lifeguards straightened the various storage sheds filled with sports gear, swim fins, wetsuits, and life vests, cleared the beach of any rubbish that might have washed ashore overnight, then paused to enjoy a few minutes of silence and sunshine before their real work began. Iridescent dragonflies supplied air cover, snatching midges and mosquitoes in midair.

Ellie was out on the lake when the first guests arrived, flying over the waves with the wind in her face, her ponytail streaming behind. How could anyone feel depressed on this glorious summer day at the most beautiful place in the world? She was a lucky girl with a fascinating future before her. She didn't need a man to complete her; she was a complete person with much to offer the world.

It was all true. Her feelings didn't respond to her own voice charms, but who could deny the truth? She lifted her chin and put Omar out of her thoughts.

This lasted until close to noon, when she noticed a guy on a single water ski fly up the ramp, stick a perfect landing, then shake a fist in triumph. A trick skier with brown skin who looked like Omar. But he couldn't be Omar. Had one of his brothers arrived? She slowed her scooter to watch.

While the ski boat raced across the lake, the skier did numerous front flips and side flips off its wake with perfect control. Definitely Omar, she decided, and he was even better than she'd remembered. He must have been skiing at other venues all these years. As the ski boat passed her position, she vaguely recognized its driver as Torbjorn, the fish guy. Where was the spotter? There didn't seem to be a . . . An instant later she sat upright on her scooter with a jolt. A *man* was driving the ski boat and heading straight toward the island! The buzzing sound in her head . . . Sirens! She must stop him! She must—

The skier flew high into the air, lost his ski, did a spectacular aerial cartwheel, and landed hard on the water. "Omar!" she cried, and her scooter was in motion. All thought of Torbjorn and sirens had fled. The water around Omar seemed to boil as something huge passed below.

"No!" Ellie cried in horror. Omar had popped to the surface and was upright and conscious, paddling with his arms and staring about with wide eyes. Ellie was racing toward him, calling his name, when a huge, weedy-looking head rose from the water just ahead.

She had to turn her scooter aside and drop her speed. The lake serpent turned toward her, revealing strange yellow eyes with slitted pupils and a mouthful of dagger-sharp teeth. Then it arched out of the water with its mouth agape and crunched down on something floating on the surface. The water ski!

Turning back to Ellie, the monster grinned wickedly, waggled its ears, flicked its tail out of the water some distance away, and sank beneath the waves. It must be near forty feet long and very powerful. It might have broken Omar's back with a flick of its tail. It might have bitten him in half . . .

"Ellie!"

She spun on her seat and saw him swimming toward her, buoyed yet hampered by his life vest. "Omar!" she cried in relief and stopped her scooter to let him close the gap rather than risk running him over. His eyes were huge, and he scrambled up behind her so quickly that she had no time even to offer him a hand.

There was no blood. He seemed well and whole. Prince Omar was seated behind her on the scooter and soaking her with cold water! Life was suddenly very good. Ellie felt quite fond of the lake serpent.

"Are you injured at all?" she asked, amazed at her own outward composure.

"N-no." His teeth were chattering. He was shaking all over, and she saw gooseflesh on his brown arms. "Ellie! Ellie, I . . . I . . ." He fell silent, apparently at a loss for words.

Immediately she strove to calm him. Forget the rules; Omar needed comforting. "Those were some amazing stunts, especially the jump off the ramp.

I can't imagine why the lake monster knocked you down, but at least there's no other harm done. Well, except to your ski. I'll drive around until we find it—what's left of it—and you'll soon dry off and warm up." She was babbling, but the charm worked anyway. As it always did.

Omar sat up very straight behind her and didn't seem to know where to hold on. She wasn't sure how to tell him that he should hold onto her. But for now it didn't matter; she was merely coasting about in search of his ski. Which they did locate, neatly snapped in half with no ragged edges. "Now why would the monster destroy your ski?" Ellie wondered aloud as they picked up the halves.

He said nothing. She laid the pieces across her lap and was about to tell Omar to hold on, when the water boiled up and something struck the scooter from below. Ellie lost her seat briefly but caught the handles and pulled herself and the ski pieces back in place just as she heard a splash behind her. "Omar?"

He was in the water again, looking more nervous than ever. This time he accepted Ellie's hand but mostly pulled himself up. "Hold on to me," she told him firmly. He immediately wrapped his arms around her, and his cold, wet legs pressed against hers.

Big mistake. She could hardly remember how to make the scooter go.

Omar could hardly believe he was clinging to Ellie. She was sun-warmed and smelled amazing, and she was in his arms . . . somewhere inside her life vest.

Amid all the crazy results of his decision to ski on Faraway Lake again, this one outcome made the risk worthwhile. Ellie had told him to hold on to her, and he was not about to make her say it twice. Her ponytail blew into his face, and he closed his eyes and tried to hold on to the moment.

The scooter slowed. Omar opened his eyes. They were still out in the lake, far from the docks and facing the island. "Oh no," Ellie said.

"What?" he spoke almost into her ear.

She hesitated, then said, "Your driver. He beached the boat on the sirens' island, and I can't see him anywhere. He must have gotten out and walked away. I don't think anyone has ever done such a thing before. I'll have to go or send someone to get him."

Just then, something slimy rose from the water and brushed Omar's ankle. He let out a yell and jerked his leg up, nearly capsizing the scooter. Too late he realized that his scream had sounded disturbingly like one of Rita's.

Ellie turned, shifting on the seat and pulling out of his grasp to fix him with a direct stare. "What is going on? Why is the lake serpent tormenting you?"

Omar felt his face go hot and hoped she wouldn't notice his blush. "It hates me because my brother Hachim and I once surprised it while it was sunbathing. It looked so funny floating on its back with its white belly reflecting the sun and a big smile on its face."

"You laughed at the lake serpent?" she asked, her eyes wide, remembering her encounter the day before.

He nodded, holding her gaze, noticing flecks of blue and green in her silvery eyes. "Then it capsized our canoe. We had to swim ashore, thinking all the time it was going to eat us, but it only knocked us around a bit. It was a long walk back to the castle. That's why I haven't gone near the lake in years. It always knows and stalks me. I used to have nightmares that it would come after me on land."

She gazed into his eyes a moment longer, searching, wondering. "Then why did you go skiing today?" Her voice was quiet.

His heart pounded so hard, he was afraid she would feel it through their lifejackets. "Because it was the only way I could be near you."

Her lashes fell, hiding her eyes, and pink bloomed in her cheeks. She suddenly turned and leaned forward, opened a small compartment in the scooter's dashboard, and drew out a familiar spray bottle. She propped it on her knee and waited.

Omar studied her in profile, her smooth forehead, her cute nose, her full lips and determined chin. What was she thinking? Would she ever speak to him again? Had he driven her away with his blunt honesty?

When the monster's spiky, dripping head broke the surface, mouth agape to show all its ugly teeth, Ellie was ready. She sprayed it right in the mouth with her potion, replacing its fishy breath with fresh peppermint. "Monster dear, you must leave Prince Omar alone now. He has learned his lesson and is sorry for ever teasing you. He knows now that you are a magnificent creature to be feared and revered, never mocked."

The monster closed its mouth, apparently to ponder the minty flavor. Its eyes still glittered, but it appeared open to suggestion. Ellie nudged Omar's lifejacket with her elbow. "Apologize now," she whispered.

"Ah, um, yes. O great monster of the lake," he began, "I apologize for my rude and unkind behavior to you. I was an insolent and foolish boy with no respect for those older and wiser than myself. And handsomer," he added. "Please forgive me."

The monster's rounded ears and fleshy beard twitched, and its uncanny eyes seemed to study Omar's face in search of hypocrisy. Omar held his breath. Then its nostrils opened wide and blew out a misty breath very like a sigh. It blinked once at Ellie then swam off, making perfectly spaced loops of its body above the surface for some time before diving out of sight.

He watched tension drain from Ellie's profile. "That was a lovely apology," she observed. "I think you're forgiven."

"I think that monster likes you," he responded. "It would never have forgiven me if you hadn't told it to. And it was showing off for you there at the end."

A smile crept over her face, and she gave him a twinkling glance over her shoulder. "It was, wasn't it?" But then she stowed away her bottle and revved the scooter. "I must get you back to shore and send someone after your driver."

"The sirens won't hurt Tor, will they? He's king of a strange agent; he spends his life studying or working. The guy knows everything there is to know about fish. But he's a good friend."

"No, the sirens won't hurt him, but they don't need encouragement. The last thing we need is for one of them to fall in love with him. Hang on."

Omar wanted to ask what would happen if a siren fell in love with a man, but he held his tongue, resumed his grasp around Ellie's life vest, and stared at the back of her neck with her ponytail whipping his face until they approached the dock.

Two other workers were there to meet them and tie up the scooter, including the supervisor, Bence, who gave Omar a hand but ignored Ellie. "What happened?" the man asked gruffly. "Why did the lake serpent attack you? Are you injured, Your Highness?"

"I'm not injured," Omar said. "The serpent didn't hurt me." He turned back to give Ellie a hand, but she was already on the dock and walking away. He shoved his way through the frightened, curious, excited crowd to reach her side. She was talking with three other lifeguards, with her back to him. He wanted to touch her arm but didn't dare. Instead he spoke firmly. "Ellie?"

She turned, and for an instant he saw her eyes brighten, but then her face went still and she spoke quickly. "Your Highness, I am thankful you're unharmed. We're making plans to rescue your friend now." Then she turned back to her coworkers, who stared at him with eager curiosity.

Omar spent the next several hours repeating the story of his rescue. Again and again, to lifeguards, the resort director, and the staff psychologist, he told everything that had happened (except the details most important to him, of course) and emphasized Ellie's heroic role.

Later, in private, he would recall every detail of Ellie's face and voice, and the feel of her—and her lifejacket—in his arms.

CHAPTER SIX

ENCE WAS HAVING CONNIPTIONS BY THE TIME Ellie finished her report. At first the supervisor intended to go to the island himself and "drag that bird-brained lord back to the castle," but everyone on his staff, male and female, declared this a terrible idea.

"We'd then have two siren-crazed men on our hands," said Kerry Jo, a bubbly blonde lifeguard with a deep tan. "Not a pretty picture."

"Fine. Then you'll go, and Ellie and Jeralee. But all of you remember: This guy is breaking rules right and left, interfering with magical creatures. I don't care if he is a lord; use your magic on him if you have to." He glared at each of them in turn. "Now I get to go inform Madame Genevieve that we allowed male guests to steal a ski boat and invade the island."

As Bence stormed away, Jeralee muttered, "Good luck with that," and flashed Ellie a grin. The magical mechanic was short and strong, with a mop of red-brown hair and a freckled nose, and she'd been Ellie's best friend since their first summer as interns.

Out on the docks, the three girls prepared for their mission. "What if the sirens won't give the guy back to us?" Kerry Jo asked. "How do we negotiate? Do we have any authority over them?"

"We'll manage," Ellie said, feeling a touch of soothing magic slip past her guard. "We should take two scooters, leaving one of us free to drive the boat back, if it still runs."

"I'll get it running," Jeralee interrupted. "If the propeller is wrecked, I'll use magic."

"I met this guy Tor yesterday," Ellie admitted, "and he seemed harmless enough. He caught some boys fishing and took their gear away. But he wasn't mean about it, just firm."

"I think I saw the fish man," Kerry Jo said. "Tall

with buzzed hair?"

"That's him."

"I escorted those boys to Madame's office," Jeralee said, and grinned. "They told me the weird guy has a pet catfish in the lake. Seriously?"

Ellie kept her opinion to herself. "I'll do my best to keep Tor under control," she said. "The sirens stopped calling, so we can hope he'll be back in his right mind."

"Yeah, like that's ever happened," Kerry Jo grumbled. Her own magic was weak—she used it mainly to keep her hair neat or hide blemishes—but she never seemed envious or resentful. Many of the staff guys cherished unrequited crushes on her while she blithely played the field, but she was also kind-hearted and worked hard.

Jeralee rode on the back of Kerry Jo's scooter, and it was agreed that Ellie would circle the island alone in search of Tor. She first escorted her friends to the beach, where they could easily see Tor's footprints on the slope of sand. "Seems so wrong to set foot on the island," Jeralee commented, "but what else can we do?" Kerry Jo kept her scooter in idle while Jeralee ran ashore.

"The footprints look as if he headed north, or

maybe straight across," Ellie said. "If I find him, I'll send him back here, so be on the lookout."

Jeralee was checking the boat's propeller when Ellie drove off. There was no sign of the fish rescuer on the rocky cliffs at the island's north end, so she hurried around to the west shore across the island from the beach.

She saw Tor's colorful life vest first; he was waist-deep in the lagoon. A mermaid with long blue-black hair hovered in the shallows right in front of him. They seemed to be having a conversation, which was odd. But the siren heard Ellie's scooter, turned to stare with wide dark eyes, then dived back into the lake and was gone. Only after she disappeared did Ellie think of speaking to her.

"Kammy!" Tor called after the siren, his voice strained. "Don't forget!"

"Stop, Tor!' Ellie put power into her command, and not the soothing kind.

He stopped, and the light faded from his expression. Ellie immediately felt guilty, but what else could she do? This situation was unlike anything she'd ever heard of.

"Tor, walk to the ski boat, push it into the

water, and ride with the lifeguard to the docks. Once you get there, people will tell you what to do next."

His chin lowered. For a moment Ellie feared he was fighting her, that she might have to use stronger magic to keep him under control. But then his shoulders drooped, and he walked slowly out of the water and up the beach. Ellie climbed off her scooter, hauled it above the water line, and followed him. She had to be certain her control held long enough to get him off the island. The sirens might start singing again at any moment.

But he made it back to the boat without incident. Never once looking at any of the girls, he pushed the ski boat back into the water.

"Thank you," Kerry Jo said in her cheery way. "We couldn't budge the thing without you."

He slightly ducked his head but still didn't make eye contact. Maybe the siren spell was still on him? Ellie wondered. Her own spell shouldn't make him depressed. "Climb aboard," she ordered. "Kerry Jo will drive the boat now." Again he obeyed without a word or glance. Once seated in the back of the boat, he leaned forward with his head in his hands, his shoulders slumped.

The three girls exchanged looks. "Will you be all right?" Jeralee asked Kerry Jo, who shook back her hair and grinned.

"We'll be fine, me and Fish Man. You take good care of my scooter." She started the boat, backed it with expert skill, and carefully threaded her way between the rocks that dotted the small bay. Jeralee followed in her wake.

Ellie looked at the pristine tropical island around her and paused. Despite its beauty, something about the place sent a chill down her spine, as if hidden eyes watched her and disapproved. She deliberately turned and walked up the slope of sun-warmed white sand. A breeze brushed her face, and the nearest palm trees waved ever so slightly. Her steps sped up, and then she was sprinting back to her scooter. It started at her first try, and she gunned the engine. Once out of the lagoon, she glanced back, half expecting to see something watch her departure. The lagoon was peaceful, idyllic. The small beach was empty. Nevertheless, Ellie shuddered. The sirens' island wasn't evil, but neither was it friendly.

She drove around the south end of the island,

near the flat-topped rock where the sirens usually sat to preen and sing. It was empty. Had Tor's landing on their island frightened them away? She jetted away across the lake, eager to put distance between herself and the island.

As she approached the docks, she caught a flash of iridescent blue tail in the water. The little siren must have followed the boat carrying Tor. Could the strange magical being truly care for a human man?

Ellie didn't know what might happen if a siren and a human fell in love, and she had no desire to find out. Maybe the Gamekeeper would know what to do. She needed to ask him the next time he came. She was beginning to think he needed to come soon.

❦

The following morning at breakfast, Ellie and her friends received a summons to an emergency staff meeting. Only the human and dwarf staff members were required to attend, the brownies having no interest in such things. As entirely volunteer employees, they were free to come and go as they pleased. They never pleased to go, which worked for everyone. The hobgoblins were freeloaders, allowed to stay because it wasn't worth the effort to send them away. Besides, Geraldo and his kin had lived at Faraway Castle for as long as anyone could remember, and no doubt much longer.

Staff meetings took place in the large lecture room next to the director's office. The two entry doors were at the front of the room on either side of the lectern, and the rows of folding theater seats rose toward the back of the room, meaning that no one could arrive late or sneak out without being noticed by every person in the room. Madame Genevieve sat in her usual place in the front row, where she could observe and direct the proceedings.

Ellie was not at all surprised when the meeting turned out to be a discussion of the previous day's events. Bence, the lake supervisor, gripped the lectern with both hands while he opened the meeting with a rundown of the situation. "We lost a rowboat to sirens last week, and now, not only was our most expensive boat taken out by two young men," he said, "but safety standards seem to have been ignored. Where was the spotter? Our policy is no fewer than three people in a ski boat, at least two of them being responsible adults, and the driver a female."

There was shuffling of feet and averted eyes among the staff, but no one spoke. Bence continued, "I understand that this week's fine weather has greatly increased the number of guests at our lake, but safety must always come first. Our two patrollers were out on the lake, one at each end, but where were the lifeguards on shore?"

Ellie's old friend Savannah raised her hand. "We must have been setting up for the children's birthday party when those men took the boat. None of us saw them take it."

Madame Genevieve suddenly rose and stepped forward, and Bence deferred to her. She took his place behind the lectern and scanned the crowd of summer workers with a grand air. "I first must inform you all that Lord Magnussen has been examined by our magical psychiatrist and found to be in good mental health. He was administered a palliative injection and will be under observation for the next few days. It need hardly be said that he is banned from the lake until further notice."

It took Ellie a moment or two to realize that this Lord Magnussen person was Tor. What, exactly, was a palliative injection? Was it a placebo or a tranquilizer?

"It is unpardonable to suggest," continued the director, "that a noble guest of the resort, let alone a royal guest, could be to blame for this catastrophe. If our staff members cannot take responsibility for their own actions and failures, they will not long be employed here. There were twelve people working at the lake yesterday; all of them will be fined a full day's pay. Perhaps then we may avoid such oversights in future. And for a patroller to allow this guest to drive a ski boat all the way to the island and run it ashore—this is beyond the pale."

She leveled her stern gaze at Ellie. "You. Miss Calmer, did you or did you not see the ski boat pass you with a man at its wheel?"

"I did," Ellie said.

"At what point did you realize that the driver was a man?"

"The boat was approximately three hundred feet from the island."

"Why did you not pursue it and prevent the

driver from running it ashore? You had plenty of time to do so, from all accounts."

"I was rescuing the skier, who had been knocked down by the lake monster," Ellie said. "He seemed to be in the most imminent danger. I thought he might be unconscious or wounded."

"The serpent has never harmed a human," Madame said, her manicured fingernails tapping the edge of the lectern. "Yet you decided the guest in the water was at greater risk than the male guest driving a boat directly to the island?"

"I did," Ellie answered firmly.

Madame looked satisfied, as if she had carried an important point. "You will remain here to fill out all paperwork regarding the accident and your actions. And when you are finished, you will work today at the riding stables, not the lake. This meeting is over."

Her chin went up a notch, and she left the room.

A troubled buzz started as soon as the door closed behind her. Several of Ellie's friends gave her commiserating glances as they moved toward the door, and Bence stopped beside her chair to assure her that she had done everything right.

Ellie tipped her head back to meet the supervisor's gaze. "Why does she blame me for this, Bence? I know she's never liked me, but really?"

He folded his arms and looked grim. "You know how she does sometimes—takes a particular dislike to a female staff member, especially if a guest pays attention to the girl. It tends to build over the course of a summer and then *boom,* the girl gets fired. It's happened more than once during my years here. You've been here a long time, so I doubt she would fire you, but I recommend you lay low for a while and let her attention and anger shift to someone else."

"How can I do that and still get my work done?" Ellie asked.

Bence shook his head and said, "That's a tough one." Which answer was no help at all.

Ellie spent the rest of the morning filling out paperwork about the accident and her actions, wondering how any of it could be useful. If the guests were never at fault even when they broke the rules, how could a staff member ever be right? She wasn't seriously worried, since the Gamekeeper had long ago made clear that Ellie worked directly under his authority.

But Madame could certainly make her life more difficult.

CHAPTER SEVEN

ELLIE ATE A QUICK LUNCH IN THE STAFF DINING hall with Jeralee and Rosa, who both ranted quietly about her public reprimand. But the situation was too painful and puzzling for her to discuss easily. "You two are the best," she said sincerely as she rose to carry her tray to the counter. "I really do appreciate your support."

Rosa nodded. "We understand. When and if you're ready to talk about it, we'll be here."

"She won't dare fire you, Ellie," Jeralee repeated for at least the third time. "You work for the Gamekeeper."

Ellie tried to smile. "Hope you're right. See you later. I've got to report at the stables."

At least, she thought while taking a shortcut through the garden, she enjoyed working with horses, though she wasn't much of a rider. The three dwarfs and two brownies who ran the stables were her old friends, so this "punishment" assignment should be enjoyable.

A few hours of shoveling manure and toting carts of muck outside to dump on a compost heap gave Ellie plenty of time to think. Perhaps a few days of stable work involving no contact with Prince Omar would allow Madame's displeasure to fasten on someone else. One could hope.

She enjoyed listening while Cog the stable manager, Tea, his wife, and their son, Kai, discussed the arrival of new foals. Horses shifted in their box stalls, and through the open barn door she could see others grazing peacefully at pasture. A sense of deep contentment pushed worry from her heart.

Then a message came from the castle: Six hunters were required for a cross-country outing in thirty minutes.

The dwarfs hopped to work, and Ellie

scrambled to help groom and saddle the horses. Like most animals, horses responded well to her soothing magic, so she enjoyed renewing her acquaintance with a sweet chestnut mare called Solvig and a handsome bay gelding known as Dustin.

Just as Kai led out the sixth horse, the riding party arrived, four men and two ladies, all dressed in fine riding attire and safety helmets. Ellie scanned them with little interest until a face caught her eye. Prince Omar looked particularly classy in buff breeches, a black polo shirt, and a glossy pair of riding boots. And on either side of him, Raquel and the Honorable Gillian in chic, snug-fitting jackets, jodhpurs, and boots.

Suddenly short of breath, her stomach aching, Ellie ducked behind the horse closest to the stable, hoping to slip inside unnoticed. But just when she reached the doorway, a familiar voice said quietly, "May I have some help over here?"

She slowly turned. The others were all mounting up, but Omar stood beside the tall gray, his expression somewhere between respectful and hopeful. "I seem to have a problem with the bridle."

"Of course." She hadn't tacked up this horse, but she still might be useful. When she approached, Omar handed her the reins, put his hand on the bridle's cheek strap as if he were showing her something, then leaned close and said, "I hear you're in trouble about yesterday. Is there any way I can fix it? You were in no way at fault."

She shook her head. "Bence says I need to keep my head down for a while. Which means not socializing with guests. I thought you would be at the lake today."

His expression made her knees melt. "I was, but you weren't there," he said. "So now I'm here, and today is no longer a total loss."

"Omar!" Raquel's sharp voice called, startling Ellie so that she jumped and had to stop herself from looking around. "Hurry up! We're ready to ride out."

He held Ellie's gaze one moment longer, touched her fingers when he took back the reins, then leaped up on his horse, swung his leg over, and settled into the saddle in one continuous motion. "Sorry," he said to the group. "Something needed fixing."

And the entire group rode off, hoofbeats thundering nearly as erratically as Ellie's heart. Did she welcome further attention from Omar despite the director's warnings? Yes. Emphatically, yes.

Cog started assigning work. "Kai," he said, "you and Ellie clean the nursery barn."

Oh joy. More manure.

Kai was a sweet young dwarf near Ellie's age, but he always clammed up around her. Shy, no doubt. Today she wished he were more of a talker, for shoveling out stalls occupied her body but not her mind, and her thoughts tended to run in dizzying circles. What could she do to prove her competence to Madame Genevieve? Did Omar truly care for her, or was he merely flirting? He had always seemed more studious than flirtatious, but maybe he had changed during the past year.

Within the hour, they heard a shout from outside. "Are they back already?" Ellie asked.

Kai looked puzzled. "We didn't expect them for another hour at least."

They laid aside their rakes and hurried outside to see the entire group enter the stable yard, several of their horses lathered and wild-eyed. The mare Solvig was riderless, while another carried two people: Gillian perched behind Omar on his horse, her arms around his waist. As Ellie hurried forward with the others to take reins and calm the agitated horses, she saw Omar jump down from his horse and reach up to help Gillian down.

Ellie felt slightly sick. Why had Gillian been sharing his horse?

The members of the riding party all seemed to talk at once. With some difficulty Ellie discerned that they had encountered something frightening. She was too busy calming poor Solvig to hear what that something had been.

"You're all right," she told the mare, slowly drawing closer as the terror faded from the horse's eyes. "You're safe here, sweet girl, and whatever frightened you is far away now. You have a clean stall and a snack of fresh hay waiting for you in the rack." Cautiously she reached up to stroke the mare's sweating neck then scratched between her jawbones. When Solvig stretched her neck forward to enjoy the scratching, Ellie knew all was well. She straightened a flaxen forelock over Solvig's pretty white blaze and let the horse bump her shoulder with a soft pink nose.

Tea spoke just behind her. "That girl was cruel to her. Look at the blood around her mouth." She took Solvig's reins. "Thank you for calming her. Some of the others need your help too." The dwarfs were short, yet the horses responded better to them than to most humans, Ellie noticed. Kai had a particular connection with the great beasts.

Both Omar's mount and Dustin seemed tired but calm enough, so she moved on to the other three horses, soothing and encouraging until all were placid and cooperative. Omar and the blond young man who'd ridden Dustin worked alongside the dwarfs to care for the horses while the other four riders stood across the stable yard. The two men conversed quietly, but the girls had no filters.

Gillian's voice was at least an octave higher than usual as she described her ordeal. "I shan't sleep a wink tonight, I know! The monster leaped out at us, and that horrid beast I was riding dumped me into a clump of little pine trees, and my new jodhpurs are covered in sap. Look at them! Quite ruined! Then the beast refused to let me mount again, and everyone kept shouting at me."

"Because you were a complete idiot about

handling that horse," Raquel remarked with a wry smile, snapping her boot with her riding crop.

"I was not! It was a terrifying experience. I could have been killed! All of the horses were frantic, and I was nearly paralyzed with fright."

"Paralyzed people don't wail like banshees," Raquel put in.

Gillian continued without pause: "But then Omar drew me up behind him on his horse, and I felt safe." She cast an adoring gaze Omar's way, but he was bent over, cleaning a rear hoof of the "horrid beast," and didn't seem to hear.

Lady Raquel told her to please be quiet, sounding even sharper than usual. "One would think you'd encountered a werewolf or dragon, the way you go on. It was only a unicorn, Gillian."

A unicorn. They had encountered a unicorn on the mountain! Forgetting her pride, forgetting all else, Ellie hurried over to question the riders. "Please tell me about the unicorn. Where did you see it, and what did it do?" she asked, carefully keeping magic compulsion out of her voice.

The two girls stared at her.

"Where did you come from?" Raquel blurted.

Gillian looked her up and down. "You are

always dirty. Why should we tell you anything, Cinder Ellie?"

Before Ellie could respond, the blond boy joined the group and answered her questions. "Gillian wasn't jumping today, so she was on the bridle trail alongside the eighth jump, a double gate, when her horse shied and tossed her. I thought I saw something pale in the trees and rode closer to see."

"Beside the eighth jump," Ellie repeated. "Go on. What did you see that identified it as a unicorn?"

His brows jerked upward, but he continued: "It charged my horse then vanished behind a bush. Everything happened fast, but I remember the horn and the wild eyes."

Raquel spoke directly to him, placing her shoulder between him and Ellie. "I thought it seemed lethargic for a unicorn, Your Highness," she said. "I've seen one before. This one seemed slow."

This blond boy was a prince? No wonder Raquel was being territorial.

"Nonsense," Gillian snapped. "It was crazy and dangerous! It would have killed me if not for

Omar." She turned and again gazed toward Omar with dewy eyes. He rubbed down a tall bay mare, apparently oblivious to the entire conversation.

"All resort guests are given a button to push, on a wristband like this, if they're ever threatened by a magical creature," Ellie said firmly, displaying her receiver. "It transmits location. One of you should have thought to use it."

"Is that what the wristband is for? I got one, but I left it in my room," the prince confessed with an apologetic smile. "I'm new here. Sorry!"

"A stupid wristband wouldn't have helped us fight off a crazed unicorn," Gillian scoffed.

"I never wear mine," Raquel added. "Unless it transforms into a magic sword for fighting off monsters, I don't see the use."

"Its use lies in bringing help to wherever the magic creature is." Ellie stood firm. "A unicorn can be lethal if it feels threatened. Usually they are gentle and reclusive, not aggressive."

Raquel said with a low chuckle, "The girl who catches cinder sprites thinks she knows all." Turning again to the blond prince, she asked, "Would you like to join my family for dinner tonight, Your Highness? I'm sure you know many people here, but no one would appreciate your company more than your own nobles."

"Thank you, my lady, but I already have dinner plans." The prince was polite yet cool, and Ellie thought she detected a faint hint of irony in his tone. After giving dismissive little bows to Raquel and Gillian, he turned to Ellie.

Amid the jumble of emotions emanating from the group of riders, she sensed nothing from this prince. Ah, so he was magical too! How powerful was he? She casually probed around . . . and felt a jolt, like an electric shock in her mind.

His silvery eyes glinted in amusement. "I apologize for the oversight regarding the wristband, Miss . . .? I don't believe I've heard your name."

Ellie was too surprised to speak. Had he stopped her from prying into his magic? How?

"She's just a worker here, and a know-it-all," Raquel informed him, then turned a jealous eye upon Ellie. "She has no authority over us whatsoever, Your Highness."

The other two men now stepped over and joined the group. "There's no need to send any messages. We can handle one unicorn, I should hope," the one with a thick black beard stated. "We'll put together a hunting party and handle the beast."

"No!" Bristling, Ellie looked this man straight in the eyes, for she was his equal in height. "You will not search for the unicorn, and you certainly will not capture or kill it. Magical beasts on Faraway Castle property are off-limits to all guests." She struggled to hold back her magic, feeling ready to burst with it.

And felt a gentle restraint, like a hand on her shoulder—only it was inside her mind.

The bearded man glared back at her with ice-blue eyes. "Who are you, girl, to order me around? I am Maximilian of Petrovce, Crown Prince and Guardian of the Realm."

Yet another arrogant prince. Ellie wanted to roll her eyes.

Raquel laughed. "She is Cinder Ellie, trapper of cinder sprites and garden imps."

Ellie sensed a reassuring presence behind her just before Omar spoke. "As Controller of Magical Creatures on resort property, Ellie Calmer possesses authority to protect her charges from all guests, royal, noble, or otherwise." His quiet voice carried a note of finality that impressed the others, for, aside from Gillian's murmured complaints and Raquel's murmured orders to shut her mouth, no one said another word.

Most of the party left soon afterward, giving up on Omar. The blond prince—whose name she still did not know—gave Ellie a parting promise. "I'll keep an eye on ol' Max, and from now on, I promise to use my wristband if there's a problem with a magical creature."

"Thank you."

She sensed friendly approval like a pat on her shoulder . . . though he merely bowed, gave Omar a knowing look, and walked after the others.

"Who is he?" she asked. "I don't remember seeing him before."

"Can't remember his name right off, but he's from Auvers. A good kid. He's grown up a lot in the past few years." But Omar sounded distracted, and she knew he intended to talk with her.

Ellie turned to untie Dustin's lead rope, focusing on it instead of meeting Omar's eyes. "Thank you for standing up for me just then. My position doesn't tend to garner much respect from guests."

"They get my blood up, the way they talk about you. And to you. It's just wrong," he growled.

Seeing Omar angry was a new experience for Ellie. Angry on her behalf, even. She wasn't sure what to say. "Thank you for caring." She shrugged. "It doesn't change things, but it matters to me."

"I care a lot more than that, Ellie."

He followed her as she led Dustin into a box stall, but she turned on him before he could enter behind her. "Your Highness, you say you care, and you asked how you might help me."

"I do, and I did."

She saw the truth of his words in his eyes, which made it harder to continue. "I must tell you that my contact with you twice this week has caught the director's notice. The rules about fraternization with guests are strict, and the lake-staff supervisor thinks Madame Genevieve may be looking for a reason to fire me. I'm not sure she has that authority, but . . . Please, please . . ."

She didn't know quite what to ask of him. Did she really want him to leave her alone? "If I were to lose this position, I don't know what I'd do. I mean, the resort is my home now."

He looked crushed. "I didn't know. I'm sorry. I'm truly sorry."

"It isn't your fault, really."

"The ski-boat incident was. Tor wanted to take the boat, and I went along with him and skied without a spotter. I knew the lake monster hated me, and we both knew the sirens would call. We were irresponsible, and you're taking the blame. It isn't right."

Ellie's brows drew together. "Did you hear the sirens?"

"I heard something, but I was too intent on showing off for you." His boyish grin and honesty were contagious, but she resisted.

"You heard the siren call," she repeated, "and it didn't affect you? How can that be?"

He looked baffled. "Maybe I wasn't close enough? Maybe they aimed their song at Tor since he was driving."

Ellie could only shake her head. "Are you sure you don't have magic?"

"If I do, I'm not aware of it. Tor doesn't have magic either."

Ellie removed the horse's halter then stroked his smooth side while he pulled straw from a rack.

"Tor is kind of . . . different, isn't he?"

Omar stood just inside the open stall door, several feet away. "I see him now and then at school—he works at a private ocean-research lab in Barbacha, near the university. He's working on a doctorate, and he travels a lot. But I met him first here at the resort years ago—he came twice, I think—and yeah, he always was unique."

"Crazy about fish?" Ellie smiled at him over her shoulder.

"He used to be crazy about birds, but that changed." His face brightening, Omar leaned against the doorframe. "He's my brother Taim's age, and I tagged along with that group when I was a kid. Tor's from Hyllestad, way in the north, and his father is a greve."

"What does that mean? It sounds like a kind of bird."

He chuckled. "A greve is the equivalent of a count or earl. But Tor cares little about politics or society." Omar spoke easily, sounding more confident than she'd ever heard him outside of statistics or calculus discussions. "He's got more brains than should rightfully fit into one man's head."

"You should talk, Mr. Mathematician."

Omar looked sheepish. "I'm sure he's smarter than me. I'm not sure what brought him back to Faraway Castle after all these years. He's close-mouthed about his personal life."

"Interesting," Ellie said, trying to process this new picture of the panfish champion.

"Hmm. Not too interesting, I hope," Omar said.

She glanced up and caught a warm, teasing glint in his eyes. Immediately she focused on smoothing a section of Dustin's mane. The stall seemed small and intimate, and she heard no other voices in the stable. The horse let out a long breath and shifted his weight off one rear foot, eyes half shut.

"Where will you be working tomorrow?' Omar asked. "I will be discreet, I promise. More than anything, I want to be near you, Ellie. I've wanted to know you for years now. Do I annoy you? Tell me honestly if you've had enough and wish I would fade into the woodwork."

He sounded so vulnerable. She believed he was sincere. But . . . he was a prince!

Ellie shoved her shaking hands into her coverall pockets and turned to face him with the solid warmth of the horse at her back. "I don't think you should follow me, Your Highness. I . . . I can't . . ."

He swallowed hard. "I'm moving too fast and scaring you. I'm no good at this. I don't know how to talk to girls. Not about anything that matters. I never really wanted to before." That quickly his demeanor changed back to self-conscious uncertainty.

She took a quick step toward him, saying, "No, no! You're not the problem. I mean, not the real you. But you're a prince, and I'm . . . I'm Cinder Ellie, the sprite wrangler." Her hands flew up in frustration. "Omar, please go away!" But her voice betrayed her by breaking.

Renewed hope burned in his eyes, and he bowed gracefully. "As you wish. Until we meet again, Ellie Calmer."

Ellie closed her eyes and clenched her fists until she knew he was gone. Then she let out a long breath. The more time she spent with Omar, the more she wanted him near . . . and the more complicated her life became. If he took her seriously and stopped coming around, she thought her heart might break. But it had to happen sometime—there could be no future together for a prince and a cinder-sprite wrangler.

Time to concentrate on important matters. Such as contacting the Gamekeeper.

❧

That evening, back at her cottage, Ellie pulled a tiny silver tube from her pack, opened one end, and spoke into it. "Guests encountered a unicorn today near the cross-country course. I have a dozen sprites and two imps. Please come soon." The Gamekeeper would understand the urgency of the situation when he heard her message.

As soon as evening darkened to night, she stood at her cottage door and gave a churring trill. Another trill echoed hers, and a shadow flitted past her through the open doorway and perched on the back of a chair.

The nightjar messenger and the magical speaking tubes had been provided to her by the Gamekeeper himself, and using them never failed to make her feel privileged and important.

She held up the tube. "To the Gamekeeper, if you please." The bird made no objection when she slid the tube into a ring on its leg. "Thank you," she said.

It bowed its head briefly, then opened its pointed wings and darted away. She caught only a glimpse of it against the sky before it disappeared into the night.

CHAPTER EIGHT

OMAR'S RAMBUNCTIOUS SIBLINGS OFTEN HAD dinner in the family suite under their nanny's strict eye, allowing their parents and Omar one peaceful meal in a day. On this evening in the dining hall, Omar picked at his food while conversation buzzed around him, hearing nothing except highlights of his conversation with Ellie, seeing only the encouraging look in her eyes as they spoke in the stable, tasting only the sweetness of her face and voice.

More than ever before he believed she was the girl for him. Strange how he'd known before they shared even one real conversation. Over the years he had observed her, slyly asked questions about her, and admired her character and reputation as well as her undeniable beauty. He'd spent a lifetime surrounded by pretty girls, enough to know that physical beauty could never be enough. He wanted a lifetime mate he could respect and love, a friend and companion.

"Omar?" his mother said.

He realized tardily that she had spoken his name several times already. He blinked out of la-la land and into reality. "Yes, Mama?"

Then he realized that people, two of them ladies, stood beside their table, and he quickly rose, nearly tipping over his chair. The Earl and Countess of Roxwell and their daughter, the Honorable Gillian, greeted him with glowing smiles. A premonition hit him like a fist to his stomach.

"Lord and Lady Roxwell have invited us to their suite this evening, wishing to honor you, Omar," his father said, evidently pleased and proud.

"To . . . honor me?"

"For your fearless rescue of our precious daughter," said Lord Roxwell through a broad smile. His lordship's hair was red-gold like his daughter's, but there the resemblance ended. No doubt to Gillian's relief, she was in all other respects the image of her beautiful mother.

There was further talk, but Omar, drowning in a sea of denial, heard nothing more until his mother spoke the fatal words: "We gladly accept."

Afterward Omar was not altogether sure he hadn't let out a whimper of horror. If he did, the noise of the dining room swallowed it.

As soon as the earl's family departed, with Gillian casting Omar backward glances filled with promise, Queen Sofia tried to rush King Aryn through his dessert and brandy. "We mustn't keep them waiting, dear." Then she turned to Omar, squeezed his forearm, and laughed in delight. "What exactly happened today? How could you keep something like this from us, Omar? You never said a word!"

"I said nothing because it was nothing, Mother. A unicorn frightened Gillian's horse, which dumped her into a copse of little trees. She's never been much of a rider. She was screaming and swearing and couldn't seem to move, so I hauled her out while another fellow caught her horse." He rubbed his sweaty palms on his thighs, desperately hoping they believed him. "But then she was hysterical, and her horse wouldn't let her remount, so I let her ride behind me. That is the full extent of my heroism, I assure you."

Queen Sofia's pleasure dimmed. "Omar, it isn't like you to speak ill of a lady. She must have told her parents flattering things about you, for they seem quite eager to befriend us."

The evening went downhill from there. As they walked to the castle's west wing, his parents seriously discussed the potential political advantages of an alliance with the island duchy of Roxwell, a manufacturing capital with financial and political ties extending over the entire northern continent.

And the visit with Gillian's family only deepened Omar's distress. Her parents urged her to relate her version of the adventure, which bore scant resemblance to his own: The unicorn had been huge and fanged, its horn and eyes glowing red, and Omar had dashed under its very nose, lifted the helpless lady into his arms, and snatched her away from certain death. Strong implications of passionate embraces and declarations of undying love laced every word.

Omar was hard put to keep his jaw from dropping at the lies. Nothing he could say dimmed the gratitude or determination of either set of parents, and Gillian glowed with adoration and triumph.

The visit lasted under an hour, but the king and the earl managed to imbibe a quantity of port while Gillian and the two mothers spoke of family traditions, travel, and fashion. Omar received the distinct impression that his mother wished to regard Gillian as a daughter, and his father seemed quite chummy with the fish-eyed earl by the time Omar helped him out the door and through a maze of halls to their own rooms.

Omar slept little that night. When morning dawned he was wide awake, staring over the edge of his bed at the place where Ellie had sat looking up at him only days before. The day his life equation started to become rational and real.

She was the only woman he would ever marry. That much he knew for certain. If anything, events of the previous night had cemented his decision, providing a stinging eyeful of the life he could end up with if he didn't stand firm.

He flung himself out of bed, glanced out the window to see clear skies, and threw on running clothes. Some of his best thinking happened while running, and he could use a brainstorm or two.

A few minutes later, as he entered the lobby, he noticed someone else heading out the main doors, a guy in running gear. There were plenty of running trails, so not a problem. But this person turned, saw him, and waited for him to approach. "Omar. Want company?"

"Sure, why not?"

It was the prince from Auvers who'd joined the riding party yesterday. He was young—eighteen or nineteen? But he looked fit, and he'd done his part helping with the horses after the disaster ride.

They decided to run one of the trails beside the lake. "No more than four miles for me today, and slow," Omar said. "I need to work back up."

"Good with me, as long as we can do a few sprints."

"What's your name again? Sorry I can't remember."

"No big deal. It's Briar."

They jogged on a path leading west along the

lakeshore between flowerbeds and green lawn. A stand of trees blocked the lake from view. Everything seemed idyllic, yet Omar felt uneasy. "Do you ever get the feeling you're being watched? I mean, like, now?"

"Watched by what, flowers?" Amusement laced Briar's voice, and Omar was about to subtract the kid from his potential-friends list . . . but then Briar glanced at him. "To be honest, yeah, I do. This place is laced with magic. I'm only half kidding about the flowers."

"When did you arrive?" Omar asked.

"Night before last. Seems like a great place."

"You haven't been here before?"

"Never, but I've heard about it all my life."

Conversation lagged, yet the silence was comfortable. Trees still blocked their lake view, but the snow-topped mountains rose above all, majestic and silent.

"Something wrong?" Briar asked. "I don't mean to pry, but you seem out of sorts."

"Parents pushing for marriage," Omar said. "Wrong girl."

Briar nodded. "Understood."

No further words necessary. Then the trail cut

right toward the lake, revealing a view of the sirens' island . . . or where it should be.

Omar nearly tripped over his own feet. "Whoa, look at that!" The lake shimmered in morning sunlight, but a thick mist enveloped the island.

"I'm guessing the fog is unusual," Briar said.

"Very," Omar said.

They both stood there, panting.

"Magical, of course," Briar said calmly. "The island has sirens, I've heard."

Omar gave his head a shake. "A friend of mine drove a ski boat to the island the other day and walked up the beach. No human has ever done that before. I'm guessing the cloud is connected to Tor's island invasion. Sort of a message from the siren queen to keep off."

"Took a lot of nerve to try a stunt like that." Briar's silvery eyes glinted as he surveyed the island. "Fantastic. That island . . . it doesn't belong here, does it."

"They say the siren queen moved it here from Singkiang."

Briar shook his head in wonder. "I really want to see this place."

"It's off-limits to guests."

Briar glanced at him. "We'd better get going."

A feeling of something wrong hovered over Omar all the way to the two-mile marker and remained after they turned back. Briar was a good running partner. He talked enough, but not too much. Yet Omar sensed impending trouble, and he feared Ellie would be involved. Was Briar connected with it?

After a furtive glance at the blond prince, Omar tried to remember what he knew about Auvers. It was a wealthy land with extensive coastline and many harbors, ruled by a queen with a prince consort. He thought there was some tragic story connected with the Auvers royal family, though he might have gotten his northern countries mixed.

When it came right down to it, Omar didn't know much about any of his summer companions. In his experience, relationships formed at Faraway Castle seldom went deep, although his sister Layla seemed happy in her marriage to a lord from El Dabaa, an ancient land far to the west of Khenifra. The two had met at the resort every summer, and somehow during the eighth year something had clicked for both of them.

Friendships were difficult enough for Omar. Romance was a greater challenge still, but he was highly motivated. If Ellie needed help or protection, he wanted to be there for her.

He and Briar sprinted the last stretch then agreed to cool down by walking to the docks and maybe even taking a plunge. Now that he'd apologized to the lake serpent, Omar thought he might take the chance.

While they paused at the picnic tables to stretch, a noise caught Omar's attention. On the shore near the beach, someone was putting a kayak in the water. The guy climbed in, pushed off, and Omar saw him clearly.

Tor.

Taking a kayak.

To the island. The island covered in magical mist.

Omar spun toward Briar. "That's Tor. He must be siren enchanted. We've got to stop him." He took off running along the shore, shouting, "Tor, don't do it! Wait—you don't know what you're doing!"

Tor heard him. He shook his head and paddled faster.

Omar stopped beside the row of upturned kayaks and stared, his mind racing. What could he do? If Tor entered that mist, would he ever return? Old legends spun through his head. Tor might go insane. He could be dragged under and drowned, or even eaten by sirens!

Briar appeared at his side. "What should we do? Was he wearing a lifejacket?"

"Yes. He swims like a fish. But the sirens . . ." He made up his mind. Turning, he gripped Briar's forearm and pushed the button on his wristband. "That calls Ellie Calmer, the girl from the stables yesterday. She might be able to talk Tor out of the enchantment. Go back to the castle—she'll find you. I'll take another kayak and chase Tor down."

He flipped one upright.

No paddle.

He took off running toward the storage sheds and racks.

"But won't the sirens enchant you too?" Briar ran beside him.

"I don't think so." Omar snatched a paddle off a rack and ran back. "Go get Ellie!"

"Right. Be careful." Briar headed off toward the castle.

Omar shoved his kayak into the water, climbed in, and started paddling. Tor had a big head start, but there was still a chance.

CHAPTER NINE

I N THE CASTLE BALLROOM, ELLIE CAREFULLY HERDED a flock of cinder sprites into a corner where she had sprinkled fresh spinach and romaine. Two males and five females, one of these quite pregnant, squeaked and puffed, but she heard the occasional crackle.

"Look at all those lovely greens I brought for you," she crooned while pulling on her fire-resistant glove. "And there is more good stuff in my comfortable cages. Wouldn't you like to join a whole herd of sprites at the Gamekeeper's castle? Imagine a world where sprites run free . . ." She couldn't help grinning when one of the females suddenly bucked and squealed then ran ahead into the waiting feast.

"There now. Smart girl! What did I tell you?" Once the creatures were happily tucking in, she could freely walk among them, tempt one at a time with a carrot, and lift it into a cage. The process took time, but she was patient. Her goal was always to capture the little squeakers without one of them going ember, and in the quiet of the ballroom she had a chance for complete success.

Her wristband buzzed. Frustrated, she glanced at it. Someone near the docks. It couldn't be cinder-sprite trouble—they mostly avoided water— and the lake monster wasn't a real threat. Could it be sirens? She looked back at the cinder sprites and shook her head. Whatever it was would have to wait until she finished this job.

The big black-and-white male would be the challenge. He had led his friends into the promised land called Ballroom and to all appearances expected to take over the place, though what he thought they would eat, Ellie couldn't guess. Sprites were hard to figure sometimes. Her magical urgings had confused this tough guy into compliance, but she recognized a battle going on inside his tufty head with its long, spiraled horns. He could prove a challenge to capture.

"Here you go, sweet little thing," she cooed to the uncertain expectant mother, whose hair fell over her face in a peekaboo style, as she lifted her into a cage. The sprite took one look at the pile of kale waiting for her and started munching with contented little grunts, her slender horns bobbing as she chewed.

Only the big male was left, but he eyed Ellie and the cage waiting for him with deep suspicion. He was a particularly handsome fellow, but she deduced he wasn't the brightest intellect among sprites. Even sprite girls sometimes fell for the big, handsome, dumb ones.

"Hey, gorgeous," she said, holding out apple slices in a fan shape. "I've got something special for you."

The sprite stood on his tiptoes in front, nose high and twitching. Ellie nearly laughed at his expression but wisely stifled her mirth. He took a few steps forward, paused, looked her over with his big eyes, and dared a few more steps. Just as he took the first nibble, someone burst into the ballroom and shouted, "Miss Calmer? Ellie? Are you here?" Then his eyes alighted on her with relief. "I used my wristband. Didn't it work?"

The big cinder sprite squawked, crackled, and burst into flame. The magic glove protected Ellie's hand, but the apples sizzled. To her shock, the hissing ball of fire's glowing red eyes fastened on the encroaching human, and it lowered its horns and charged. Ellie snatched up her spray bottle and shot its backside with the first stream. With one surprised squeak, the sprite melted into a large puddle. Relieved yet irked, Ellie turned on the intruder.

He stood still, eyes twinkling. "Nice shot," he said before she could speak. "You rescued me." Only a hint of sarcasm colored that smooth voice. She recognized the blond prince from the riding party. He was dripping sweat and panting.

"What are you doing here?" she snapped.

"Omar told me to get you," he said, and raised his hands defensively. "Hey, like I said, I tried the wristband button."

Her attitude crumbled, and her heart jumped to her throat. "Omar! Is he all right? What's happened?"

"We got back from a run and saw a guy named Tor taking a kayak to the island. Omar went after him, hoping to make him turn back."

She sucked in a sharp breath. "I've got to go after them both. Have you told anyone else?"

"Not yet. Omar told me to find you first."

Ellie set down the spray bottle and peeled off her gloves. "I must tell the lake supervisor; I can't just go off on my own. Will you please scoop up that sprite and put it into this cage? Be gentle."

He looked from the blob of goo to the tiny cage to Ellie. "You're kidding, right?"

She wanted to laugh at his expression, but the situation was too grave. "Just do it." And she left the room at a run.

She found Bence at breakfast in the staff dining hall and apprised him of the situation. He leaped to his feet, sent a page to inform Madame Genevieve, then set off running with Ellie. "You say Prince Omar went after him? Then we're likely to lose two kayaks and have two ensorcelled men on our hands," he groused. "Take a scooter and see if you can catch up with at least one of them. I would act as backup, but I can't approach the island. I'll send help as soon as possible."

Not even Madame could find fault with Ellie now that she was acting under Bence's orders. She sprinted down to the dock and was soon skimming across the smooth water on her scooter. The island was shrouded completely in a weird fog, and there was no sign of the two young men. They must have entered it.

"Your Highness!" she called, her voice sounding thin. "Prince Omar?"

Silence. She stopped outside the fog bank and tried to use her magic to discern its nature. She sensed anger in the mist but nothing worse. "Omar?" Saying his name bolstered her courage. Slowly she drove into the fog, calling again, but she heard only waves slapping against rocks.

Then the water around her scooter began to dimple and boil. She scarcely had time to panic before a huge, weedy head rose from the water beside her knee. A yelp escaped before she registered what she was seeing. "Monster! Have you seen Omar or the other prince?"

It waggled its ears and bumped the scooter, shoving her to the right, then submerged and appeared ahead of her. Trusting its guidance, she followed slowly. Rocks loomed out of the fog on all sides. Sharp rocks that could destroy a boat or scooter.

"Omar?" she called again.

This time a male voice answered, muffled in the mist.

"Omar!" Slowly she followed the monster's spiky head. Every rock made her heart leap; every dark wave looked like Omar's hair. "Omar, where are you?"

"Here! Ellie?"

"Yes, I'm Ellie. Keep talking so we can find you."

"Glad to. You have no idea how good your voice sounds to me."

A moment later the lake serpent submerged, and Ellie saw the prince bobbing in the water, the orange of his lifejacket muted in the fog. "There he is! Oh, thank you for your help, dear serpent!" she called, even though she could no longer see the monster.

Its tail tip flickered above the surface a few feet away.

"Omar, are you all right?" Would he recognize her? Or would he steal her scooter and desperately try to reach the sirens?

He spun about to face her, and his brilliant smile flashed for an instant. "Ellie!" Then he was swimming to meet her. She was so happy that she almost forgot to offer him her hand, but he climbed up easily anyway. He wore running gear, complete with sodden shoes. The seat of her coverall soaked up the streams of water running off him, but she, at least, had had sense enough to change into water shoes.

"Are you all right? What happened?" She half-turned, trying to face him, and the idling scooter bobbed in the water and scraped against a rock. Then something pushed it from below, and they began to slowly move through the water, weaving between rocks. Trusting the serpent, Ellie sat sidesaddle on her scooter and focused on Omar.

His hands gripped her shoulders, and he studied her face as if his life depended on memorizing it. "I'm all right," he said slowly, "though my head feels weird, as if something is buzzing inside. I think there must be magic in this fog."

"There is magic, but I don't think it's evil. I suspect the siren queen is angry about a human walking on her island." But Omar was acting . . .

strange.

He slowly lowered his forehead to rest on her shoulder and heaved a deep, shaky sigh. "Ellie. Don't leave me."

"I won't, Omar." She allowed a tiny amount of magic into her soothing voice. "You'll be fine now."

She felt the tension leave his body. "Thank you," he said hesitantly. "I feel better already."

"I'm glad." She should probably have asked him to sit upright, but she didn't.

A few loops of serpent body appeared behind the scooter. Rocks slid past in the fog; waves from the scooter's passing lapped against them.

"Did you ever find Tor?" she asked.

"I did. He wouldn't stop, so I chased after him into the fog. He told me to go away. Said the sirens weren't calling him; he came to find a friend. But his eyes were dilated . . . He looked seriously crazed." Omar shook his head. "I couldn't make him hear sense. When I wouldn't leave, he tipped me out of my kayak and smashed it over a rock."

"What?" Ellie gasped. "You mean, he picked it up and—"

"Yes, he did. Dumped me out, hoisted it over

his head, and smashed it against a rock until it was in pieces."

Ellie's heart raced. "Is he nearby? Did you hear the sirens call?" She kept almost seeing things in the fog. Her eyes flitted from rock to rock.

"I never did hear a siren this time, but the fog makes my head feel thick, like it's stuffed with cotton. Maybe it affected Tor too. I don't know what to think. I didn't see him all day yesterday, and now . . . He looked drugged, but maybe that's what siren-enchantment does. What man could be friends with a siren?"

If Tor had been enchanted, then why wasn't Omar? Ellie pulled slightly away from him, and when he lifted his head, she peered directly into his eyes and reached up to touch his cheek, feeling the morning stubble. "You know who I am?"

He blinked in surprise. "You think I'm siren addled? I'm not." His smile was weak but genuine. "Ellie Calmer, magic-creature wrangler."

"We must get Tor back, but I can't fit both of you on this scooter with me."

She had just decided to take Omar back to the dock and return for Tor, when the quick *glub-glub-*

glub of a ski-boat engine reached her ears. Relief nearly melted her limbs. "Somebody's here." She faced front, and Omar rested his head on her shoulder from behind.

The lake monster's tail touched Ellie's leg in a clammy caress. It gave the scooter one last push then vanished beneath the surface. "Thank you," Ellie said quietly.

Moments later, the scooter slid ahead into blinding sunlight. Ellie shaded her eyes with one hand and looked around. Not twenty feet away, a ski boat idled in the water with Madame Genevieve at the wheel.

"Miss Calmer, is that Prince Omar with you?" she called across the water. "Is he enchanted?"

Omar lifted his head and shaded his eyes. "I'm not enchanted," he called back, "but I don't feel so well. I think Tor is on the island. He dumped me in the water and wrecked my kayak. He said he wanted to see a friend. One of the sirens, I guess. Please let me get away from here," he added with feeling, then again lowered his face to Ellie's shoulder. He touched only her life jacket, but she saw Madame's lips tighten.

"The fog seems to contain a mild repellant, but

aside from a headache, His Highness is fine." Ellie tried to sound businesslike and efficient.

"Miss Calmer, take Prince Omar to the castle at once and deliver him to the magical psychiatrist for professional evaluation."

"Yes ma'am. Oh! And I sent for the Gamekeeper last night regarding the unicorn incident. He will be here this evening, in case you need his help with the sirens."

If anything, Madame's expression darkened, and she muttered something like ". . . the last person we need . . ."

Ellie gunned the scooter's engine, and Omar tightened his grasp. Ahead, the lake and Faraway Castle looked completely normal. Behind, the ski boat vanished into the wall of fog. She felt Omar sit up and look back. Then his arms slid around her, and he leaned close.

"Strange," he said. "I feel better already."

The scooter slowed slightly. Ellie couldn't help herself. "Your headache is gone?"

"It is, though I still feel as if I'm in a dream. Ellie, while I floated there, I could think of nothing but you. Everything about you. And then you appeared out of the fog." His voice was low and intense. "I feel enchanted, but you're not using your magic. Knowing you is the best thing that's ever happened to me."

She could not speak or move. The scooter slowed to a crawl then stopped there in the middle of the lake as she turned her face slightly toward him. No dream could equal this moment.

"However, I realized while I was floating in the fog that I know almost nothing about you." His voice became more practical but no less urgent.

Against her own better judgment, Ellie laid her arms over his, wrapped around her waist. "You know everything that matters." She suddenly felt guilty, defensive, and frightened. His sweet words couldn't begin to touch the barriers between them, and she was a fool to let them melt her. But oh, being in his arms felt so good!

"True, I know all the things that matter most, but I'm missing your history. Where do you live when you're not at Faraway Castle? I want to meet your family."

"I have no family," Ellie said. "I was raised by a burva who taught me how to use my magic. I live with Arabella when I'm not working here." Her voice sounded normal though her emotions were in turmoil.

"Your parents?"

"I think they are dead." But her voice held a question, because her mind had always held that question. Arabella never would talk about Ellie's family or history. When asked, she always said that Ellie knew. But she didn't.

The mood was shattered. Just as well. She revved the engine and drove directly for the dock. Omar shifted slightly away. "Have I offended you?" he called against the wind. "Please forgive me."

"Nothing to forgive," she shouted back.

Omar felt Ellie's withdrawal like a physical sting. A moment before, she had melted back against him and he thought their hearts were one. Now, she was as remote and cool as the mountain peaks surrounding the resort. Why had he brought up her family just then? What a stupid thing to do! He had been thinking of how he might ask her parents for her hand, how he could best introduce her to his parents, how he would go about dropping the bombshell that he was in love with the magical-creature controller of Faraway

Castle and intended to make her his bride. But Ellie could not have followed his rambling thoughts.

He squinted at her slender neck through her ponytail, which blew into his face. She was a stranger again, and it was his fault.

A small crowd awaited them at the dock. Omar climbed off the scooter as calmly as if he had not just ruined his own life, then removed his life jacket, sat on a bench, and pulled off his soaked running shoes. He felt people gaping at him.

He looked up, frowning. "I'm not siren-addled," he said distinctly. "Madame Genevieve is rescuing Tor, Lord Magnussen." At least, he hoped she was. That woman was seriously unpleasant.

One of the lifeguards was saying to Ellie: "The director took the boat and told us to stay here. Did you find the crazy guy?"

While Ellie explained, Omar looked over his shoulder toward the island still hidden in that weird bank of fog. His obsession with her had driven his old friend from his mind for a time there. Now he remembered the agonized intensity of Tor's voice and expression. Would he, Omar, smash a kayak if someone tried to keep him away from Ellie?

"Your Highness, Prince Omar," a strange voice said, "I am John W. Smith, the resident psychiatrist. Madame the director requested me to interview you upon your return. If you will come to my office adjoining the lobby as soon as you are suitably clothed, I shall be much obliged."

Omar turned to see a man dressed in white, as if he had been called out during a tennis match, beckon with one hand. He looked back at Ellie, but she was surrounded by other staff members, answering questions as if nothing unusual had happened.

Feeling sick at heart and light in the head, he nodded. "I'll be there shortly."

When he stood up, his wet clothes clung to him like a memory of that fog, and as he walked away he heard Raquel's laugh, followed by, "Don't be ridiculous. Cinder Ellie is a nobody, an orphan. She traps pests for a living. No prince could be serious about her."

CHAPTER TEN

THE MEETING WITH DR. SMITH LASTED WELL OVER an hour and seemed pointless. Aside from a lingering headache, Omar felt fine and answered every question easily. At last the doctor leaned back in his chair. "Thank you for your time. You may go, Your Highness," he said, scribbling something in his notebook.

"Your diagnosis?" Omar inquired as he rose from the uncomfortable chair.

"Perfectly normal. I see no need to administer an antidote to siren enthrallment. Which is, in truth, remarkable. Everything connected with your siren-enthralled friend defies reason. He proved resistant to the antidote, an unprecedented occurrence. I intend to study files on the history of that island and past events connected with it, if Madame will allow me the key."

"I would be interested to hear what you discover," Omar said with minimal genuine interest. He left the office intending to return to the lakeshore in search of Ellie, but just as he stepped outside, his younger siblings approached the portico, obviously coming from the lake. "There he is!" The children shouted with delight and charged him like an army, brandishing water toys like weapons.

Rafiq reached him first. "Omar, did the sirens steal your brain?" he asked with disturbing hopefulness.

"If they did, no one has noticed a difference," he answered.

Yasmine and Rita caught hold of his hands. "We were swimming and saw you riding on Ellie's scooter. Did she rescue you again?" Yasmine inquired. "Wait until you see the picture I drew!"

"She did, and I look forward to the unveiling of your newest masterpiece."

"I got a color book!" Rita shouted, and whacked

him with her rather sandy treasure to draw his attention.

"Awesome! May I color a picture in it with you?"

"Yes, yes, yes!" She let go of his hand to dance a happy jig.

"Since Ellie's rescued you three times now, do you get to marry her?" Karim asked. "Rita says you do. But Rafiq wants to marry her, if she will wait for him to grow up."

With a gasp of inarticulate protest, Rafiq grabbed and quenched his little brother. Omar would have enjoyed this banter and roughhoused along with them had he not seen their parents approaching at a more measured pace. "Hush now," he said, still grinning.

But when he looked up again, the Honorable Gillian and her parents had appeared behind his own. His grin froze and wilted. Premonition of trouble pinched his stomach, but he greeted the entire group politely.

The queen spoke first. "Children, go inside and find your nanny. Yasmine, watch Rita."

Rafiq gave Omar a pitying look, gathered up his siblings, and escaped indoors. Then Queen Sofia turned her tender gaze upon her older son.

"Omar, dear Gillian has told us of your very difficult situation, and we are resolved to approach the resort director to demand resolution."

Omar looked to his father for an explanation, but the king, a man of few words, nodded agreement with his wife. "Let us move away from the doors here," King Aryn suggested, and led the group toward a ring of benches surrounding a firepit near the covered boat landing.

Only Queen Sofia and the countess sat down. Gillian hovered behind her mother and tried to catch Omar's gaze.

Omar had followed his parents, but he was in no mood to tolerate Gillian's games. "May I ask what situation concerns you?" he asked, trying to catch his father's eye.

"This must be terribly trying for you, Omar dear," the countess said before the king could speak, "but it should be easily resolved." Her face, as pink-and-white and lovely as Gillian's, expressed sympathy.

Omar glanced from face to face and guessed they must be talking about Tor's flight to the island. He propped one foot on the side of the firepit. "Actually, my part is over," he said, "so there is no need of intervention. Madame Genevieve herself is even now resolving the problem, and I suffered no ill effect."

"The resort director is involved?" the king asked with evident surprise.

"Yes, I saw her myself on her way to the island."

"On her way to the island?" the countess said. "Why would she go to the island?"

"To resolve the problem, as I said." Omar held out his arms to display his undamaged condition. "As you see, I escaped unscathed from the sirens, aside from a headache and wet clothes. How that happened I don't quite understand, but I'm not complaining!"

"Sirens," the queen said, looking puzzled. "What are you talking about?"

Omar met his mother's gaze, equally puzzled. "This morning's emergency. The difficult situation. My friend, Lord Magnussen, who ran away to the island? It's all resolved now. He smashed my kayak and left me floating in the lake, but one of the staff members picked me up, and here I am. No harm done."

Queen Sofia glanced at Gillian. "I had not heard of this trouble. Our concern is this servant girl who keeps throwing herself in your way. The situation, left unaddressed, could damage your reputation."

"Servant girl?" he echoed. "I don't know what you're talking about." His gaze alighted on Gillian, who gave him a gooey smile. Realization arrived, with horror on its heels. Omar's mouth dropped open.

The king spoke in his quiet way. "Your mother refers to the young woman known as Cinder Alice who follows you everywhere."

"Ellie. Cinder Ellie," Gillian corrected bluntly. "It is completely obvious that the girl is throwing herself at you, Omar, probably hoping for money. Everywhere you go, she shows up. At the lake, in the castle, at the stables—she is a stalker, and you're too naïve to see it."

Omar laughed. He couldn't help it. "Miss Ellie Calmer rescued our entire family from cinder sprites the morning after I arrived," he told his parents. "Sunday, she pulled me out of the lake after the lake monster knocked me off my skis and then persuaded it to stop harassing me. Today, she pulled me out of a dangerous situation yet again." His anger burned hotter with every word he spoke, yet he kept his voice down. "In the past few days she has rescued several other people, including Lord Magnussen. She has been doing her job, following the director's orders."

Now furious, he turned on Gillian. "Did you make up this story about Miss Ellie to try to get her fired? What reason can you possibly have for slandering a poor working girl? She didn't make you look foolish yesterday on the riding trail; you did that to yourself."

Gillian gaped, then gave a treble roar of rage. "Oooh! How dare you! I hate you!" Ending with a pitiful wail, she covered her mouth with one hand and ran under the portico and through the castle doors.

The countess rose to stand beside her husband. Drawing himself up to his full height, the earl took a step forward and addressed King Aryn and Queen Sofia. "All wedding plans are off until your son apologizes to our daughter." Then, united in outrage, he and his wife followed Gillian into the castle lobby.

Knowing the worst was yet to come, Omar

braced himself.

"Omar, how could you make such a scene?" his mother asked in a stage whisper. "Where are your manners? Where is your self-respect? Do you wish to cause an international incident?"

"I am not the one who shouted," he pointed out firmly. "And if those people intend to start a war based on their daughter's lies, they are unworthy of political leadership."

His mother paused, blinking, her expression startled.

His father glanced around. "Rather than display our disagreements in public, we should retire to our suite. I do apologize for this unfortunate public confrontation. It was ill conceived."

The apology softened Omar's expression. He nodded and followed his parents into the castle and up to the royal suite, maintaining a polite distance as they talked quietly. His mother kept wiping tears from her face and shaking her head.

As soon as King Aryn opened the door to their rooms, Rita ran out, embraced the legs of each of her parents, then ran to Omar. He scooped her up into his arms, and she leaned her head on his shoulder. "I love Miss Ellie," she confided in a stage whisper. "She herds cinder sprites. Do you love Miss Ellie?"

Grateful for the moral support of this small ally, he put his mouth to her ear and whispered, "Yes, but it's our secret, okay?"

Bright-eyed and smiling, she nodded then giggled.

Carrying his baby sister, he followed their parents along the hall. Just as he entered the family sitting room, Yasmine rushed in, waving a paper which she handed to him with great pride. "See? It is you and Miss Ellie!"

Karim hovered behind her, jumping in excitement.

King Aryn sat in a comfortable chair, one ankle crossed over his knee, while his queen gracefully reclined on a sofa beneath a huge picture window overlooking the lake. Rafiq watched over all from a doorway.

Omar looked at the drawing and felt his stomach turn over. It was a brightly colored and highly detailed drawing of a smiling, yellow-haired Ellie holding a glass cage containing a smiling cinder sprite in one hand . . . and Omar's hand in the other. He was colored brown, with black hair and a huge white smile. Pink and red hearts floated above their heads. Additional furry cinder sprites cavorted around their feet; two were tiny balls of fire with red eyes. Squiggles of smoke rose from a black blot on the ground. "My baby sprite," Rita said, pointing at the blot.

"That's really great, Yasmine," Omar said, trying to sound appreciative.

He folded it, but too late. Their mother reached out both hands. "Come and tell me about your picture, Yasmine."

The little girl eagerly reclaimed her artwork. Nestled against her mother's side, she explained each detail. "This is Miss Ellie after she saved us from the cinder sprites. These are the sprites, see? One is in the cage, and these two went ember, and Ellie already sprayed this one. And . . . and we all wish she would marry Omar, because she is so kind and pretty."

"And she herds cinder sprites!" Karim added from his current position, head-down on the rug with his feet on the sofa.

Rafiq, better attuned to the current parental wavelength, groaned softly.

Queen Sofia looked from the drawing to Omar to her husband in visible dismay.

King Aryn cleared his throat. "Children, please return to your nanny. Mama and I wish to speak with Omar alone now."

"Awww, we always have to go to Nanny at the interesting time," Karim whined, but scrammed at a glance from his father.

Omar lowered Rita to the floor, and she caught his shirt, stood on tiptoe, and planted a wet kiss on his cheek. With another beaming smile, she trotted away.

All too soon, Omar stood alone before the King and Queen. All three looked intensely uncomfortable until his father spoke quietly. "Tell us the truth about this young woman, Omar. I hope you did not lie to us."

Omar drew a deep breath. "Everything I have told you is the truth, but not the whole story. Ellie Calmer has never stalked or annoyed me in any way. I am the one who has, for the past few days, tried to be wherever she was working."

"But why, Omar?" His mother was near tears. "You, of all people, a womanizer! I would never have thought it."

"Mama, I am no womanizer," he protested, stung. "What have I ever done that you would think the worst of me? I would never insult an honorable young woman like Ellie. Neither would I disgrace my family."

"Then why seek her out, son?" his father asked.

Omar stood as if frozen. He knew the answer but wasn't yet ready to share it with his parents. Ellie should be the first to know. Or the second, since Rita already knew . . .

The king and queen exchanged a glance, and she nodded. King Aryn sat upright, straightened his broad shoulders and spoke in his usual rather formal manner. "You are now twenty-one, the age at which a Zeidan man traditionally chooses a wife. Your mother and I had thought you would wish to marry the earl's daughter, who is both beautiful and eager, but last night we detected a lack of enthusiasm in your manner toward her. After this morning's altercation, I believe we both better understand your opinion of the young lady."

The Queen caught Omar's eye and nodded with apparent sympathy.

"We bring our children to this resort each year largely for socialization—for where but at Faraway

Castle can be found a finer selection of noble and royal young people gathered in one place? You have had many years to observe the eligible young women of your age. It is time to make your choice. The annual Summer Ball will take place at the end of this week. If you will choose your wife by that evening and her parents are amenable, we will announce your betrothal that very night. Your mother and I do not intend to be dictatorial—you may choose your own wife. But she must be of noble or royal birth."

Omar could think of no response. He had never felt more miserably unhappy.

"Omar dear," his mother said, rising from her seat to place one slender hand on his arm, "although Gillian's deportment leaves much to be desired, her friend Lady Raquel might suit you, and she is also quite stunning. Her father is a mere viscount, but her blood is very good on both sides. My grandmother came from Auvers, you know. And these are only two of the lovely young noblewomen you have associated with these past ten years and more. Can you not think of even one among them you would be happy to wed?"

Omar swallowed hard. "I will choose my own

wife, and I will not disgrace the family," he said at last. He could not consider marriage with Ellie to be a disgrace. She was the best woman he had ever known. He had observed her from afar for several years, even before the incident with the lemonade, and had seen nothing that did not impress and attract him. Her reputation was flawless, her intelligence high, her dignity and manners equal to those of any duchess or queen. And she was ambitious, honest, hardworking, funny, virtuous, kind—in short, she was the only woman he intended to marry.

But how could he arrange for Ellie to attend the ball?

A short time later he found his younger siblings congregated in his bedchamber. They all turned to stare at him when he entered. Rafiq, who had been moodily staring out the window, blurted, "You aren't going to marry that Gillian, are you?"

"I am not. I am going to take a shower, and you are all going to vacate my room. But thank you for the moral support," he added sincerely. "It means a lot."

Yasmine stopped paging through one of his math books to ask, "How can you get Mama and

Baba to let you marry Ellie? She isn't a princess. I heard them say you have to marry someone with a title. Or at least with lots and lots of money, and Ellie isn't rich."

Omar sat on the edge of his bed, pulled off his shoes, and dropped them on the floor. "I don't know. I must think of a way to convince them, and quickly." He rubbed his temples and eyes with both hands. Behind him, Rita hopped on the bed and flopped down on his pillows while Karim swung on a bedpost.

"Go on now," he said. "Everybody, out. I'll take you star-gazing tonight if you're good all day. There should be a meteor shower."

But by nightfall he had still not thought of a way to make his parents accept Ellie. More to the point, he had not thought of a way to convince Ellie to accept him, the more pressing task at hand.

CHAPTER ELEVEN

I N THE STAFF CAFETERIA THAT EVENING, ELLIE SAT AT
a table with Jeralee, Kerry Jo, and Rosa.
Partway through the meal, she blurted, "Kerry
Jo, I've been dying to know what happened
today on the island. Where is Tor now?"

"I don't know." Kerry Jo answered between
bites. "Madame hasn't yet come back."

Ellie stared, blinking. "She is still there? On the
island?"

Kerry Jo shrugged and kept eating.

"All we know is, she isn't here," Jeralee
answered for her. "This afternoon, the fog around
the island vanished all at once, and there was

171

black smoke rising from the volcano. Ben keeps saying it can't be a volcano, but what else do you call a hill that smokes?"

"It's a volcano," Rosa said quietly. She had pushed her tray away and now played with the little vase on their table. The carnation and fern spray in it were sadly wilted.

Ellie pressed her knuckles into her cheeks, trying to think. "The sirens didn't do anything to Prince Omar. He was right there next to the island, but according to Dr. Smith, he wasn't siren-enthralled. He had a headache when I picked him out of the water, but otherwise he seemed perfectly normal."

"He didn't look perfectly normal when you brought him to the dock, girl," Kerry Jo observed with a smirk. "He looked lovesick."

Ellie didn't know how to react, but she knew her friends could read her face no matter what she did or said.

Kerry Jo rose and picked up her tray. "I'll see you all later. Devon asked me to watch a meteor shower with him from the docks tonight. Are any of you going?"

Ellie and Rosa shook their heads.

"Maybe," Jeralee said, waving a carrot stick. "See you later." She pulled her short legs up on the bench, crossing them tailor-style, and grinned at Ellie. "So your prince looked lovesick, did he?" She snapped off a bite of carrot and munched noisily.

Ellie rolled her eyes. "Kerry Jo has love on the brain."

Jeralee swallowed and waved the carrot again. "Point granted, but she's not the only person who's noticed how he keeps appearing wherever you are."

"He does have a talent for getting himself into trouble when you're near." Rosa looked both amused and concerned. She leaned forward slightly to say, "You must be careful, Ellie. You're good at hiding your feelings, but Madame Genevieve is no fool. And it sounds as if your prince is as transparent as a greenhouse."

Ellie focused on the little vase between Rosa's hands: The carnation's petals were now vivid pink, and the fern looked fresh cut.

"Would you marry the prince if his family disinherited him?" Jeralee seemed genuinely curious. "He is handsome and seems like a great guy, but his country is so different from Adelboden. What could he do to support a family? Most of these princes are layabouts."

"Omar isn't," Ellie said quickly. "He is a mathematician and has nearly finished his university studies. He works very hard, and he could get a job or teach anywhere, on any continent. Besides, I can work hard too."

Rosa looked at Jeralee. "Omar, she calls him."

Jeralee shrugged. "I told you, she's been gone on him for years."

Ellie sat back on the bench, her face flaming. "But this discussion is ridiculous. No prince would marry me."

There was a pause, and she noticed her friends watching something behind her. Rosa murmured, "Oh no!"

"What?" Ellie started to turn just as someone stepped over the bench beside her and sat down. Someone who smelled very nice and wore a t-shirt and faded jeans. Someone with intense eyes and a dangerous smile.

"Hello, Ellie. You did not imagine your evil deeds would go unpunished, I hope?"

Ellie's face went hot. "Prince Briar!" She had

entirely forgotten him. "What are you doing here?"

"Guests do not visit the staff cafeteria. Ever." The statement might have carried more weight had Jeralee not spoken in a breathless tone.

"Ah, but they do, as you witness, fair maiden, for I am a guest," Briar responded, and Jeralee's face turned red. Ellie could not recall ever seeing her cheeky friend blush before.

The prince then turned to Ellie, his gaze accusing. "I scooped up that stinking blob and dumped it into an empty cage like you told me to, and it came back to life. You did not warn me of this, and I believe I lost at least a year off my life, along with terrifying several brownies with my screams."

Ellie maintained a straight face. "The poor brownies!"

"Yes, well, they might recover eventually. Then a withered gray creature popped in and cussed me out with no regard for my sensitive royal feelings. The brownies tried desperately to hush him and finally wrapped him in what appeared to be a tablecloth before hauling him away. Still swearing, mind you."

Ellie gave up the fight and laughed. "That must

have been Geraldo the hobgoblin. He has no regard for class or rank or species."

Briar crossed his arms over his chest, lowered his chin, and gave her a straight look between thick lashes. "I took two showers before the sulphur smell faded to bearable levels. Did you ever intend to come and relieve me, or am I doomed to feed greens and carrots to those ravenous beasts for all eternity?"

Ellie sent him a penitent look. "I don't know how I could have forgotten you and the sprites, but I truly did. Did you really keep feeding them all day?"

"They are insatiable. The brownies kept me supplied. They felt sorry for me, I believe." His eyes twinkled.

Hearing a tiny sigh, Ellie glanced at Jeralee, who stared at the young prince with stars in her hazel eyes. "Oh, Your Highness, may I introduce my friends Jeralee and Rosa?" She indicated each in turn. "This is Crown Prince Briar of Auvers."

Ellie thought he winced slightly at the title before he smiled graciously and addressed each girl by name. When he said, "The pleasure is mine," Ellie believed he meant it. What a charmer!

She noticed a certain coolness on Rosa's part but set this down to shyness. Or perhaps she viewed him as a ladykiller in no need of encouragement.

"Your Highness," Ellie said, "I do thank you for feeding the cinder sprites today and for enduring horrible smells and sights and sounds. I should run to the ballroom and clean up the mess, I suppose."

When she stood up, he rose along with her, excused himself to her friends, and stepped over the bench. "I'll be glad to help you carry cages or whatever you need."

He waited while she turned in her dinner tray, then fell in step beside her, even holding the door for her. Embarrassed, she tried to think of a polite way to dismiss him. "This is quite unnecessary, Your Highness. You have already far exceeded any reasonable expectations. I was totally out of place to demand your help the way I did."

"Maybe so, but I truly don't mind," he told her with a genuine smile. "You can pay me back by telling me what happened on the lake today, since no one seems to know. Or else no one will tell me."

"I can't tell you much, since after I pulled Prince Omar out of the lake I spent the rest of the day answering questions and filling out legal forms. Again. I suppose the legal ramifications of siren enchantment might be severe, but most of the questions I answered today seemed silly and entirely unrelated to the situation."

"You are talking to a law student, Miss Calmer. Watch your language when you speak of legal forms."

Ellie laughed again and offered no further objection to his assistance. Not only might his attention help people forget seeing her and Omar together, but she found his dry sense of humor both refreshing and challenging. She related most of the morning's events to him as they walked to the ballroom, then told him she expected the Gamekeeper to arrive that evening. "He usually meets me at the castle after dark—I think he checks in with the director—so I should wait around here. The brownies often tell me when he arrives."

"I am interested to see this Gamekeeper. But hasn't the director been away all day?" he asked as she opened the service door to the ballroom.

"She must have returned by now. Would you go and see while I clean this floor?"

"Why not?" Briar smiled, bowed, and walked away.

Ellie looked after him for a moment, frowning. Few royals possessed magic these days. She couldn't help liking him, yet she did not think he was a person she should fully trust. But then, what boy that good-looking ever was trustworthy?

Giving her head a little shake, she entered the ballroom. Cinder sprites squeaked from the cages in the corner. "Good evening, squeakers," she said, infusing her voice with happiness. "I hope you enjoyed being served by a prince all day." After checking on them, she switched on a few lights in places that didn't get natural light from the windows, took a broom and mop from the janitor's closet, and pulled out her cleaning-fluid spray bottle. Either Briar or the brownies had cleaned the floor already, but nothing eliminated a sulphur stink like her herbal spray. She mentally infused it with the scent of a mountain breeze and set to work.

When the polished ballroom floor reflected the evening's last rays of sunlight and the domed ceiling, she stopped, leaned on her mop's handle, and surveyed her handiwork. Often, while working, she forgot to notice the beauty surrounding her.

Faraway Castle was truly a worthy setting for its noble and royal guests. She could easily imagine royal balls held in this room, balls hosted by a great king, long departed. The guests would have danced to the polonaise and mazurka in huge hoop skirts. Or was the castle that old? She knew little about its history, and no one else seemed to know more.

She turned around and nearly screamed. A huge, hulking figure loomed from a shadowy corner. "Oh! Gamekeeper, I did not hear you arrive." No surprise there. He walked with the stealth of a panther.

"I entered only a moment ago." His deep voice was quiet, yet it seemed to shake the floor. He wore a hooded cape that entirely concealed his face, of which Ellie had occasionally caught glimpses and knew better than to attempt a clearer look. She was content to remain ignorant.

"Where is your wagon parked?" she asked.

"A young prince advised me to park it beside that door." He pointed to the delivery service entrance. "He told me you were here. I stopped by your cottage first and loaded up the sprites and imps. Are these cages ready to go?"

"Yes sir. I caught these sprites this morning. The big male went ember, but he seems to be recovering well."

The idea of this huge creature entering her locked cottage with no effort and removing her creatures was disconcerting, but there was nothing she could do about it except be grateful that he was benevolent.

She thought she had concealed her thoughts, but his hooded head tilted slightly. "I did not enter your home," he said.

She ducked her head. "Thank you, sir." She should have known. His magic skills were beyond anything she could guess, and during the three years she had worked for this mysterious personage, not once had he given her cause to doubt his integrity.

The Gamekeeper bent over the cages on the ballroom floor. "They look healthy and well fed. I will not disturb them now. I tend to frighten other creatures at first."

Ellie did not doubt it. He had many characteristics of a predator. His gloves could not completely hide the sharp claws within, and his feet, though booted just now, were large and wide.

"I will carry them out," she offered.

"I can help." Briar walked across the ballroom floor from the main hallway. "I met the Gamekeeper near the director's office and told him what I know of today's events."

He sounded so nonchalant that Ellie gave him a close look. Encountering someone like the Gamekeeper should affect any normal person. Briar's eyes looked wide, yet he maintained an outward show of unconcern. Bravado, perhaps.

"Has Madame returned?" Ellie asked, handing him two cages.

"Not yet," the Gamekeeper answered for him. "I will speak with her soon."

No more needed to be said. Ellie well knew that her supervisor could handle the sirens, the director, the lake monster, or any other issue or entity that might arise.

Briar and Ellie carried cages out to the wagon, leaving their arrangement to the Gamekeeper. Ellie avoided looking at her mysterious supervisor more often than necessary, so she wasn't certain whether he did this manually or with magic. The wagon itself seemed solid. Or was it? She couldn't be sure.

As they brought out the last three cages, the Gamekeeper said, "Prince Briar told me of yesterday's encounter with the unicorn. Have you any details to add?"

"One of the men spoke of hunting the unicorn," Ellie said. "I informed him that magical creatures are off limits to guests, but I'm not sure he will respect the rules. He showed no respect for me, that's certain."

"The unicorn eluded me today," the Gamekeeper said. "Wild unicorns fear me, which complicates the situation. I will return soon to seek it again."

"Do you want me to search for it?" Ellie asked. The idea frightened her, for she knew nothing about unicorns, but she was willing to try.

"Only in an emergency. And I will not hold you accountable for injured guests. Enforcing resort rules is the director's job."

"But what about the unicorn's safety?" Ellie asked.

"If you believe the unicorn is in imminent danger, contact me immediately, then do your best to protect it without risking your own safety. Although I appreciate your willingness to serve anywhere at the resort, your official position is Controller of Magical Creatures. If anyone disputes your authority or attempts to prevent you from serving as you see fit, I will intervene on your behalf." His deep voice was grave and authoritative. "Do you understand?"

"Yes sir," Ellie said. "Thank you." He could only be speaking of the director.

"Now tell me what you know about this siren situation," the Gamekeeper said. "You have twice rescued young men from the island?"

Ellie once again related her siren-related adventures.

"Was Prince Omar siren-enchanted, would you say?" asked the Gamekeeper.

"No sir. Not at all. He said he had a headache, but he knew who I was and had no desire to stay at the island or find a siren."

The Gamekeeper turned his head toward her, and she felt the weight of his gaze. Without thinking, she took a step closer to Briar, who rested one hand on the side of the wagon behind her in a subtly protective stance.

"Are you certain this Prince Omar is fully human?" the Gamekeeper asked.

"Yes." She paused. "Is it terribly unusual for a man to be immune to sirens?"

"Some enchanters can resist a siren call," Prince Briar said, as if with firsthand knowledge. If his magic was that strong, Ellie thought, little wonder he could block her clumsy efforts to probe his emotions!

"Yes. So can a man who is already deeply in love with a woman," the Gamekeeper countered, "which is less common than one might imagine."

"Oh." Ellie could only hope the dim lighting concealed the heat she felt spreading up from her collar.

Running footsteps approached, then Ellie heard feet skid on gravel and what sounded like a stifled gasp. The Gamekeeper lifted his head, looked past her, and faded away. One moment he was there, huge and looming, the next moment he was gone.

"Well, hello there, Omar and family," said Prince Briar.

Ellie turned quickly. On the far side of the delivery road stood Omar and three of his younger siblings. He was carrying Rita piggyback. All five of them observed her, Briar, and the cart with round, dark eyes, and all but Rita puffed for breath.

"What are you doing here?" Omar sounded deeply shaken.

"Wh-what was that thing?" asked Rafiq. "A monster? Its eyes glowed red!"

"Teeth!" Karim wailed. "Big teeth!"

"Where did it go?" Yasmine cried, her voice panicky.

Karim clung to Omar's leg, and Rita whimpered quietly into his shoulder, while the older two partially hid behind him.

Ellie walked toward them and used her soothing voice: "There is nothing to fear, children. The Gamekeeper looks frightening but is gentle and kind, and he will take good care of the cinder sprites for us. I caught some new ones today in the ballroom, and Prince Briar helped me carry them out here to the Gamekeeper's wagon. See the cages stacked there? The sprites we caught in your suite are here too. He will take them up to his home, where he has a safe place for all of them to live together. The mother sprite let me know that she wants to go there. I would never give our sprites to someone who would harm them. Would you like to see them?"

All four children visibly relaxed and nodded, so she beckoned them to her. Omar brought Rita then lifted her down from his shoulders, still looking wary and worried. "That was the Gamekeeper I've heard you speak of?" he asked.

She nodded shortly, gave him a warning look, and lifted a sprite from one of the cages. "Do you remember this little fellow? He is all recovered from going ember, and now he isn't afraid when I hold him. See?" She held the fluffball down at Rita's level, and the little girl gingerly touched its back then smoothed its fur. "He isn't smooshed anymore," she observed with a smile.

Behind her, Ellie heard Omar and Briar speaking but couldn't understand them at first. Then Briar said clearly, his voice edged with humor, "You're the one who sent me to find her this morning. And for my trouble I ended up scooping melted sprite off the ballroom floor. You will pay."

CHAPTER TWELVE

ALIGHT DRIZZLE WAS FALLING EARLY THE NEXT morning as Ellie began to clean out her cottage and sweep the porch and front walkway. It bothered her that someone— even a strange, beastly person—may have witnessed her disorganized clutter, so before heading to the gardens, where she had promised to help Rosa in the greenhouses, she cleaned diligently. One day too late.

Just as she finished the walkway and ducked inside to escape what was becoming a steady rain, she heard Omar call her name. He jogged toward

189

her across the grass, wearing his running gear. Even as he approached, the rain fell harder. "Here, step inside for a minute," she offered.

"Thanks." He first shook his head like a wet dog until his black hair stuck out in spikes, then stepped just inside the door, leaving it slightly ajar. Water trickled down his face and arms and dripped from his clothing. He rubbed his hands down the front of his soaking tank shirt, ruefully regarding the puddle at his feet. "I'm sorry. I wasn't this wet until I was almost here. Maybe I should stand on your porch."

He was a mess. He was every bit as sweet and adorable as his little siblings. He had been too gorgeous for words even as a gawky teen, but now he was a man. Six feet of lean, fit perfection. And he stood in her house, nearly filling her entryway. She tried not to notice how his wet shirt clung to his skin or how his eyes sought to hold her gaze. "It's all right." She sounded breathless even to herself. "I haven't put my cleaning supplies away yet."

His usual bright smile was absent. "Is something wrong?" she asked.

"The resort director is still absent, and Briar

told me this morning that he was invited to join an unofficial unicorn hunt scheduled for today at twilight. Apparently some of the lords brought rifles along even though shooting game of any kind is banned on resort property."

"What? Twilight?" She panicked but tried to hide it. "Why twilight?"

"They seem to think it will be easier to find the unicorn in the dark. Because the horn glows, or something like that."

"I suppose that makes sense . . . but men with guns in the dark makes my job a lot more dangerous." She was already planning her message to the Gamekeeper.

"Which is why we're not leaving you to deal with this alone. Briar already agreed to join the hunt."

"What?" She hardly knew the magical prince, but this felt like betrayal.

"His plan is to delay and confuse the others so that either the Gamekeeper or you and I can find the unicorn first. Yes, I'm going with you. We hoped maybe you could use your magic to persuade the unicorn to leave Faraway Castle grounds?" His voice turned the last statement into a question.

"I can try." Her brain was spinning. "I can't put you and Briar in danger."

"You're not putting us in danger. This whole plot is our idea."

Ellie's heart warmed at Omar's kindness, and his tentative smile added a few degrees of heat. She still wasn't sure what to think of Briar, but she wouldn't turn down his help. "Thank you," she said, meeting Omar's gaze. "Maybe I should refuse, but I can't stop you from joining me."

His eyes brightened. "So, what's the plan?"

"The Gamekeeper searched for the unicorn but couldn't find it," Ellie said. "If we're to find it before the hunters do, we'll have to head out this afternoon or early evening in broad daylight. If the director finds out that I walked off to hike in the forest with you, she will do her best to fire me. But the Gamekeeper promised to stand by me, and I've seen her knuckle under to him before."

She met Omar's gaze with a determined lift of her chin. "This will be dangerous, you know. I'm not sure I have the power to soothe a unicorn."

"It's worth a try. I can take you directly to where we saw it. Maybe we can find a trail."

"Probably not, after this rain. I will send a message to the Gamekeeper. I hope he can get back here in time, but if not, we'll carry out the search ourselves. Be sure to wear dark clothing so the hunters don't shoot us. And we should carry a weapon, just in case."

"I'll take care of that," he said. "And electric torches." His manner was still restrained and tentative, and she sensed his frustration, hope, and . . . longing.

Might he truly be in love with her? She ached at the sight of him and suddenly wondered how it would feel to be in his arms without two lifejackets between them. But he had not yet offered her anything, and she could never settle for less than everything.

"Where shall we meet?" he asked.

"The stables."

"I'll bring food along in my pack. Four o'clock? Five?"

"My shift ends at five, but this hunt takes precedence. Besides, Rosa won't tell if I skip out early. Will four work for you?"

He nodded. "The earlier the better, as far as I'm concerned." He paused, studying her face. "Ellie, we need to talk."

She nodded briskly to hide her confusion. "Plenty of time for that this afternoon."

Omar's dark eyes reproached her. She sensed his inner struggle, but then he stepped back through the doorway into the rain. "Hope the weather clears by then. See you at four."

Ellie closed the door behind him and wanted more than anything to sit down for a good cry. The house felt so empty with no cinder sprites in the corner . . . and no Omar in the doorway.

But Rosa would be waiting for her. Life must go on, even if her heart felt likely to shatter. She spoke her message into the tiny tube, then opened her door to whistle for the nightjar.

Rosa put Ellie to work splitting and transplanting irises in a greenhouse while rain drummed on the glass overhead. It was dirty, physical work, exactly what Ellie needed right then. Far more beneficial than a pity party.

Rosa usually kept her feelings hidden, but on this gloomy day she seemed agitated. Nearly as tense as Ellie. "Is something wrong?" Ellie asked after they returned from lunch. "I mean, not with the plants. With you."

After a long silence, when she did eventually respond, Rosa's voice sounded peculiar. "Prince Briar. Do you know much about him?"

Ellie quirked a brow. She'd heard both Savannah and Kerry Jo gush about Prince Briar being too stunning for words. Had the charmer found a chink in Rosa's emotional armor?

She said only, "I know he's funny and clever. Why?"

Scowling, Rosa ripped apart a bunch of bulbs. "There is more to that guy than meets the eye. Are you sure you don't know him from somewhere?

Nope. No chink in that armor. Ellie paused before she spoke. "I think I would remember if I'd met him before. He's . . . Well, he would be hard to forget, you know?"

And yet she easily resisted his charm. Possibly for the same reason Omar was immune to the sirens' call: Her heart was already taken.

"Forgetting him is no problem for me," Rosa said, her full lips pressing into a hard line.

Oh, really? But Ellie kept her thoughts to herself, and the conversation soon changed to less volatile topics. Ellie needed to keep her thoughts from rolling back to Omar and the unicorn search, and Rosa was always willing to talk about plants and garden pests.

The two girls worked hard until Rosa straightened, pulled off her gloves, and removed her tool belt. "I've got errands to run. It's nearly four o'clock, you know."

"Is it really?" Panic knotted Ellie's stomach.

Rosa smiled. "It really is. You'd better get going." As she stepped out the greenhouse door, she paused to call back, "Looks like the storm is over. Good luck tonight. You can save that unicorn, I know."

"Thanks." Ellie managed a grateful smile. "See you later."

While cleaning up her area, Ellie wondered—not for the first time—what vital task drew Rosa to the back of the gardens several times a day. It was more than a year now since Ellie and Jeralee, convinced that Rosa was under magical compulsion, followed her through a gate, hoping to free their friend from what must be a curse. That attempt ended badly. She and Jeralee had walked away with blistered legs, no memory of what happened, and no desire to repeat the experience.

And Rosa had bluntly told them not to try again and asked them to speak of it to no one if they were truly her friends. Something in her tone and manner convinced them, so no further attempt had followed. But curiosity was less easily quenched. Now Ellie wondered, had Prince Briar been snooping around that same gate?

Ellie had filled a backpack before coming to work, so now she simply collected it from a storage shed, slung it over her shoulder, and headed toward the stables. To avoid arousing suspicion, she hid the pack behind a stone in one of the back pastures then took a roundabout route to the remotest barn. Visiting horses was one of her secret pleasures, and the maternity barn was a favorite haunt. Here, pregnant mares were stabled at night along with new mothers and their foals.

Savoring the warm scent of hay and horse, she moved from stall to stall, murmuring love to expectant mothers. Halfway down the row of boxes she found the faithful pair of stable brownies tending a mare with a foal only hours old. "Good afternoon, Howurl and Miria," she greeted them, leaning her forearms on the half door. "How is our new mother?"

"Very well, Miss Ellie," Miria answered from her seat atop the mare's neck, where she was braiding the long black mane. "And the little one is strong and lively." Her sharp eyes reviewed Ellie in a glance. "You are going for a hike with someone?"

Ellie had expected as much from Miria, who could have made a fortune as a detective were she so inclined. "I am meeting Prince Omar of Khenifra here. We intend to search for the unicorn and send it away before a party of guests can find it."

"Ah," said Howurl, his voice deep and mournful as he brushed the sleeping foal's legs. "The unicorn. We were ordered to have five horses ready."

"Would you like us to delay the hunting party?" Miria asked. "The dwarfs will help us, I know."

Ellie only smiled. "Do as you think best. One of the party also intends to sabotage the hunt: Prince Briar of Auvers."

Miria nodded. "Ah, I would have guessed it. We know him." She and Howurl exchanged a look, leaving Ellie in doubt of their opinion of the prince. Then Miria turned back to Ellie. "We know of someone else who might be willing to help you if we ask him."

"He doesn't like humans much," Howurl said in a tone of deep woe.

"We will take all the help we can get," Ellie replied, brightening. "Can this person be ready quickly? We need to head out as soon as Omar arrives."

"I'll take you to him," Miria volunteered. After tying off the pink ribbon she had woven into the new mother's mane, she touched the mare's neck and gave a command Ellie couldn't understand. The horse immediately lowered her head, and Miria walked down her neck and jumped into a mound of straw. "Thank you, Bertinette." With her tiny hand she patted the mare's cheek.

Ellie had always marveled at the glimpses she caught of the brownies' abilities and language. These two did wonders in the stables, and the horses obviously loved them. Why brownies so enjoyed caring for the houses, beasts, and possessions inside almost any structure built by humans was beyond her understanding, but she felt increasingly grateful with each passing year.

Just as Ellie and Miria approached the open barn door, Omar entered, clad in practical clothing and boots, carrying a backpack, and looking stressed. "I had a hard time sneaking off," he said. "I think my parents have asked people to keep a watch on me. I've been checking my tail frequently on my way here and took a roundabout route, so I think I'm clear." He gave a little start, staring down at Miria. "Hello. I beg your pardon. I didn't notice you at first."

Ellie's jaw dropped. "You can see her? A brownie?"

He gave her a crooked smile. "Yes. It's been . . . an adjustment."

"When did you start seeing them?" She had her suspicions.

He raised his brows and looked uncertain. "I think I was too distracted by other things to notice at first, but . . . yesterday?"

A mermaid had spoken to him at the island, Ellie was certain. As she thought of that beautiful creature she'd seen talking with Tor, her fingers curled into claws.

"I can also sort of sense when magic is being

used, though I can't explain how I know," Omar continued. "I'm trying hard to pretend I don't see the brownies and things when other humans are around, but I feel rude."

"They understand," Ellie assured him. "This is Miria."

Omar bowed politely. "I am pleased to meet you, Miria."

The little brownie curtsied. "Your Highness," she said.

Howurl scrambled over the stall door, gave Omar a doleful look, and said, "I will check to see if you were followed. We will all help you protect the unicorn."

Before Omar could respond, he was gone.

"That was Howurl, Miria's husband," Ellie said. "From him, that was a long speech!"

Omar nodded, but a slight wrinkle between his brows revealed his uneasiness. "I'm glad to have his help, but what do we do first?" he asked.

Ellie briefly explained the plan to Omar, who nodded and turned to Miria. "Right. If you will lead the way, we'll follow."

Once she adjusted to the idea, Omar's new ability delighted Ellie, who felt as if he'd suddenly taken steps into her world. More than anything she wanted to pick his brain about what all he had seen and sensed, but that conversation must wait for a better time. Maybe never, since she was supposed to be keeping out of his way . . .

After Ellie collected her backpack, Miria led them into the forest by a nearly invisible trail, then told them to wait while she slipped into a copse of young trees. Omar sat on a fallen log and patted the spot next to him. "Might as well rest your feet while you can."

Rather than hurt his feelings, Ellie sat beside him and lowered her pack to the ground. "So you had a long day?"

There was no smile in his eyes when he looked at her. "The longest. But it is better now."

She looked away, stifling a sigh. "Good. I worked in a greenhouse all day." She wanted to bring up the topic of sirens, but this wasn't the time. Besides, even if he'd spoken with one, she hadn't enthralled him.

Facts notwithstanding, she wanted to run down to the lake and order a certain mermaid to put some decent clothes on—a gunny sack would be ideal—and keep her hooks out of Ellie's man.

If only he really were her man. If only she could lean her head against his shoulder for a moment or two . . .

"What's wrong, Ellie?" Omar asked, the lines between his brows deeper than ever. "You look so unhappy."

Miria reappeared soundlessly. She was not quite a foot high, yet beside her stood a quite hideous yellow-and-brown person no higher than her knee. "This is Tob the toadstool fairy. He knows where the unicorn is hiding and why. He cannot speak human, but he understands your speech if you speak slowly."

"Hello, Tob," both Ellie and Omar greeted him.

The fairy nodded coldly, looking only at Omar through narrowed eyes.

"He says he is doing this for the unicorn's sake. Your Highness, if you will let him ride on your shoulder, he will direct you to her." She spoke to Omar, her expression grave. "Toadstool fairies do not appreciate humor or laughter." Coming from Miria, the words were a stark warning. "And Tob disapproves of human magic, which you have a great deal of, Miss Ellie. Once he has taken you to the unicorn, he will vanish."

"We understand," Omar responded. "And we are deeply grateful for Tob's assistance."

An instant later he flinched as the tiny fairy alighted on his shoulder. Tob folded his wings and laid them flat on his bare back. At close range, Ellie now saw that the fairy wore a loincloth the same colors as his mottled skin. She dared only a glance before averting her gaze, for the fairy's expression was a few shades past belligerent. Tob ignored her entirely.

She wondered how Tob would direct them from Omar's shoulder if he could not speak. She quickly found out. The fairy unfurled a long spear with a wicked thorn tip and pointed into the trees. Omar flinched again and blinked, doubtless fearing for his eyes. He stepped forward to lead the way, and Ellie fell in behind. It was a quiet hike, both hesitant to speak for fear of offending the truculent fairy.

Following Tob's guiding spear, they hiked several miles along the side of the mountain, climbing slowly. Then they descended into a vale lush with ferns. Birches, their bark and leaves silvery in the afternoon sunlight, shaded the small clearing. Tob suddenly jumped off Omar's shoulder and vanished amid the ferns. Omar and Ellie exchanged wide-eyed looks but held their tongues. Was the unicorn near? Did it even now prepare to attack?

And then the sound of deep, labored breathing reached their ears, followed by a low moan. "Are we too late?" Omar whispered. "Could it be injured?"

Tob darted from beneath the ferns at their feet and motioned for them to follow. His manner seemed urgent to Ellie. She would have moved ahead of Omar, but he put out one arm to hold her back, no doubt intending to meet any danger first. Both grateful and annoyed, she allowed his chivalry.

They could see nothing through the ferns, so Tob was obliged to redirect them more than once. But at last Ellie saw a gleam of white hide ahead, and there the unicorn lay beneath the ferns, flat out on its side. At first, hearing another deep moan, she thought it was wounded or dying, but then its entire body strained, one hind leg lifting with the effort. She noted the bulging side, the rippling muscles, and knew in a flash.

The unicorn was giving birth.

CHAPTER THIRTEEN

T HE UNICORN LIFTED HER HEAD. GREAT DARK EYES regarded Ellie with deep suspicion and a hint of entreaty. "You poor dear," Ellie murmured, her soothing magic flowing over the laboring beast. "How long has this been going on? I know about birthing, and I carry with me an herbal spray that will help you to relax and concentrate. Will you allow me to help you?"

Sighing out a groan, the unicorn lowered her head and pawed the air with one front hoof. Ellie dropped on her knees at the creature's side, disregarding the spiraled horn so near, and dug through her pack for the right bottle. Then she sprayed her herbal potion in the air above the mother's head and continued to spray over the pearly body and legs. To her relief, the unicorn visibly relaxed and at the next contraction was ready to push.

Ellie encouraged and sweet-talked and soothed by turns, oblivious to the passage of time. The incongruity of watching this powerful legendary being suffer the throes of labor brought a sense of unreality to the entire scene. She didn't notice when Omar came or went. She didn't notice her damp knees from kneeling in the rain-soaked moss and ferns. She scarcely noticed the fading light.

At last the mother unicorn gave one final great push, and her baby slid into the world. Ellie quickly cleared the tiny nostrils and watched as the newborn began to twitch and struggle. While the mother recovered her strength, the baby flailed, thrashed, flung itself about, and finally scrambled to its feet.

"A little boy," Ellie told the mother. She had never heard the correct terminology for unicorns. Was the baby a colt or a buck kid? She saw similarities in him to horses and goats. Dainty cloven hooves and a delicate bearded chin—goat. Large, dark eyes, the fuzzy mane and tail—horse. But no ordinary animal shared this creature's pearlescent hide and ineffable grace, or the tiny nub of horn in the middle of its forehead.

The mother lifted her head and rolled upright, her sharp horn passing uncomfortably close to Ellie's face. She muttered sweet nothings to her baby and licked his coat clean.

Ellie rose and moved away, giving the little family space. Only then did she realize that twilight was fading into night. Stars dotted the open circle of sky above their fern glade, and brightness over one of the surrounding mountains revealed that the moon would soon rise. Soon the unicorn was on her feet and the baby nursed happily, his tail flicking.

When the mother looked directly at Ellie, she felt gratitude wash over her, as if the beast had spoken. Warmth and happiness filled her heart, and when Omar appeared beside her, she slipped her hand into his.

He gave it a gentle squeeze, but his voice in her ear sounded urgent: "Can they move soon, do you think? We're right next to the bridle trail and the cross-country course. We need to hide them somewhere. Just minutes ago I saw torches or lanterns about half a mile down the trail, near where we saw the unicorn the other day."

"The baby isn't yet strong enough to walk far."

"Might she allow me to carry it?"

Ellie pondered the idea, but she was too tired to think clearly. Omar's presence seemed protection enough. "Couldn't we just stay here?" she asked. "Wouldn't we be safe enough if the unicorns were to lie down again?"

"Maybe," Omar said softly, his breath brushing her ear. "You were amazing, may I say."

Heedless in her post-baby euphoria, Ellie leaned her head on his shoulder. "I didn't realize how terrified I actually was. I think it's hitting me now." He smelled and felt so good that she deliberately blocked out the rest of the world . . . until she realized that the hard lump on his side was a holstered pistol and the gravity of their situation loomed large again. "Where is Tob?" she asked.

Omar stood very still, as if afraid to move. "He disappeared as soon as we got here."

The unicorn suddenly lifted her head, her

rounded ears flicking forward. She was silvery in the starlight, clearly visible against the forest trees. Omar released Ellie's hand and moved toward the trail. "Can you convince her to lie down?" he asked, his voice low and tense.

"I'll try." Quickly, quietly, she approached the mother. "You need to lie down and . . . and try not to glow. Some bad men are hunting you. We came to warn you. If you lie down, they might pass by without seeing you."

After a moment's consideration, the unicorn stepped away from her nursing baby, folded her legs, and lowered her body onto the dead leaves beneath a thick patch of ferns. Her baby staggered over to bunt his nose against her, tried to frisk, and fell over. He lay there, his belly full, his eyes drifting shut, while his mother gently licked him. Even as the moon slid above the mountaintop, sending silvery light into the clearing, Ellie was pleasantly surprised to observe that the unicorns were difficult to see. The sleeping baby glowed softly, but his mother surrounded him with her body so that little light escaped.

After arranging a few fronds to conceal them even more, Ellie returned to where she'd last seen

Omar. At first she thought he had left them, but then he beckoned and she saw him crouched at the foot of a large tree on a rise overlooking the trail. Ellie crouched beside him, clutching her pack.

They heard a horse whinny and a man shout. Close. Too close. Ellie grasped Omar's arm. His muscles were tight; he was ready to spring. The pistol was in his hand. She let go, realizing he didn't need distraction. A gun fired nearby, and someone shouted. Omar pushed Ellie to the ground and shielded her body with his. Lights flickered through the brush, more guns fired, and several voices began to shout. Ellie and Omar lay flat in the wet leaf litter.

Then a terrible noise seemed to stop her heart, an unearthly roar that shook the earth beneath her. Men and horses screamed in terror, guns fired, and hoofbeats pounded the ground. Ellie breathed in the peaty smell of moss and earth, and she felt Omar's heartbeat against her shoulder. Not until the gunfire began had she realized how close the hunters were to their hiding place. Was the riding trail that near?

She knew the source of that roar: The

Gamekeeper had responded to her message more quickly than she'd imagined possible. Perhaps he had still lingered near the resort when she sent it. Who could know? But he had come through for them tonight.

One glance over her shoulder toward the unicorns, and Ellie scrambled into motion. The mother still crouched over her baby, but her ears were flat back, and her horn and eyes glowed red. Ellie pulled out her spray and again filled the glade with the aroma of flowering clover and grasses.

"You needn't fear," she said softly. "The Gamekeeper is an enchanted beast who protects all magical creatures. He will chase away the men who wished to harm you. And if you are willing, he will take you to a place where many of your kind live in peace and safety. I understand your fear— he frightened me too when I first met him. But now I know he is good and kind. If you doubt me, ask the brownies who live and work at Faraway Castle. Or the lake monster."

The unicorn's horn and eyes darkened and disappeared in the night. Ellie again felt trust flow toward her. The sensation was strange and gratifying. All was quiet behind her, so she dared to ask, "Once we know the bad men are gone, will you come with us to the resort? We will shelter you there in secret until the Gamekeeper can transport you to the refuge."

Sensing the creature's uncertainty, she added, "The Gamekeeper will not take you to the refuge against your will. But I am certain you and your little one will be safe with him. Far safer than you can be anywhere else in these mountains."

Again Ellie sensed the unicorn's thoughts. "You wish to wait until morning? Um, let me speak to my companion."

She shuffled back to where she had left Omar, but he was not there. "Omar?" she inquired softly, trying not to panic.

"Here." He spoke aloud from a short distance away. He sounded calm, so she pushed through the underbrush and walked down the slope to the bridle path. The Gamekeeper was nowhere in sight, but another man stood with Omar. "Briar's horse bolted along with the others," Omar explained.

"My mistake," Briar said. "I dismounted to try to distract Prince Maximilian just before the

Gamekeeper spoke his piece."

"Did you see him?" Omar asked.

"The Gamekeeper? No. It's a good thing he came when he did. I delayed and muddled things up for as long as I could, the dwarfs dawdled, and the brownies at the stable were as inefficient as a brownie can bear to be, but ol' Prince Max headed for this place like a compass arrow finds the North Pole. First one, then all four mighty hunters started shooting at patches of moonlight. I'm just glad you're safe. Omar says you found the unicorn and she's a new mother."

"Yes, and they are both doing well," Ellie answered. "Thank you for delaying the hunting party for us."

"Still, if not for the Gamekeeper, we would be in a bad way right now," Omar admitted. "Where is he? Might he be wounded?"

"I never saw him at all, but then I ducked for cover after that first shot. I'll scout around if you like. I don't like the idea of leaving a wounded compatriot behind." Briar sounded as calm and cheerful as ever.

"But what do we do now?" Ellie asked. "The unicorn asked if we might rest until dawn. It won't be a comfortable night, but we should do well enough."

"I'm afraid those men will come back to learn what terrified their horses," Briar said. "They are— or rather, Prince Max is—far more determined than I'd expected. Though what glory is to be had from killing a unicorn, I can't imagine."

"The horn is valuable," Omar added, "but none of those lords and princes should be lacking in wealth. One way or another, we must get the unicorns away from this place."

"Yes, the horn of a unicorn is valuable for its magical power." Briar spoke with his usual nonchalance, but Ellie sensed something disturbing behind his words. His following statement confirmed this: "Dangerous power, in the wrong hands."

Just as she opened her mouth to inquire further, she heard a familiar trill, wings fluttered, and something landed on her shoulder. "Well, hello!" The nightjar had never before perched on her. "Just a moment, gentlemen."

She stepped aside, carefully pulled the little tube from the bird's leg, and opened it. A voice emerged for her ears only: "Take the unicorn to the maternity barn tonight; the road there and the barn are safe. I will come Saturday at dawn to collect her and the baby, if she wishes. And if you wish, you may accompany them."

Oh. Oh my! Ellie thought. The thought of traveling to the Gamekeeper's home was both exciting and intimidating. She knew with her head and heart that he was good and would not harm her, but her gut nevertheless clenched at the prospect.

After brief thought, she sent a return message. "Will comply. Thank you for stepping in. Mother and baby are well." Even as she spoke, she wondered how the Gamekeeper knew about the baby unicorn. Had he been observing them from cover? He might be watching even now. It was not a comfortable thought.

She slipped the tube in place and said, "Please take this to the Gamekeeper." The bird gave an answering chirp and took off, instantly disappearing in the darkness.

She turned to the men, their faces like mottled gray smudges in the shadows and starlight. "The Gamekeeper says we should take the unicorns to the maternity barn tonight—the road and barn are well guarded. I don't know, but I suspect he is still here."

"Unnerving yet reassuring," Briar remarked. "Let's get moving."

Omar carried the sleeping baby unicorn, walking with its mother at his elbow where she could easily touch her young one with her nose. Ellie walked at the unicorn's other side, her pack feeling heavier than it had earlier in the day, and Briar took up the rear. Walking on the bridle path through forest and pastures, they made quick progress. The night was quiet, clear, and starry. Ellie saw a few falling stars but didn't dare wish on one.

As they approached the stables, she sensed something new: an invisible magic fence allowed them to pass through to the barns—the Gamekeeper's work, no doubt.

Mira and Howurl awaited them in the maternity barn, eager to direct them to a stall piled with fresh golden straw. Miria almost smiled, she was so happy. "We will feed and protect the unicorns, you may be sure. I am so pleased that Tob kept his promise! What a fine day this has been."

Ellie felt the unicorn summon her and hurried into the stall to calm the mother's fears. "Don't worry, you're safe here. You must have sensed the magical barrier we passed? The Gamekeeper placed it around the barns so that no enemy may enter. The brownies are your friends, and if the horses are unfriendly, they are also unable to escape their stalls. In a few days the Gamekeeper will bring a special cart to carry you and your baby to the sanctuary on the far side of the mountain, and there you may live among many of your kind and raise your young one in safety, if you choose to remain. Tomorrow, if I'm able to do so safely, I'll come and visit you here." By the time Ellie finished speaking, both unicorns were asleep, glowing softly and snuggled together.

❦

Omar leaned against the stall door, watching Ellie soothe the beautiful magical creatures. He found it difficult to believe that he had witnessed the birth of a unicorn. More fantastic still, Ellie had held his hand and rested her head on his shoulder.

That moment was past, and Ellie once more

seemed distant and unreachable, but his hope remained. It was time to open his heart and place his future on the line. In four days he had to choose a wife. He would choose no one but Ellie, whether she would have him or not.

Ellie rose, straightened, and stretched her back with a soft groan. She turned, saw Omar, and smiled. But an instant later the smile faded. He opened the stall door for her, and once she stepped through, he took her pack and offered his arm. She hesitated but slipped her hand into the crook of his elbow. "Thank you, Omar, for everything."

"I'll walk you back to your cottage," he said. "And then you must get some sleep. It has been an eventful week."

"That's for sure."

They walked in silence while Omar worked up courage. "Ellie, I need to ask you something," he finally said. She was silent, so he continued as they walked. "The Summer Ball will take place in four days. I would love to be your escort. Will you come? Please?"

A pause. "But staff members don't attend the ball, Omar. You know that."

"I do, but it's a masked ball, so who will know? Other people invite outside guests for the occasion; why can't I? You can easily blend in with the other ladies."

"I can't come, Omar."

He had expected her to require convincing. "I know that a gown might be an issue, but we can find one to fit you, I'm sure."

"I don't have a gown, but that isn't the reason I won't go, Omar."

He rushed on. "My parents told me that I must choose a wife and propose to her at the ball, and they will announce my betrothal that night. I love my parents, but I can never accept an arranged marriage to a woman I don't love. I would rather be cut off without a penny. Perhaps I could get a position here at the resort—I'm experienced at bookkeeping and finance, and I understand the business—"

"No." She stopped on the walkway before her cottage and faced him. The moon and stars cast silvery light upon her sober face; and when a light breeze blew, the pine boughs overhead sprinkled them both with needles. Ellie impatiently brushed one from her face. "Omar, listen to me: I am a working girl, a magic-creature controller, not a noblewoman or princess. I could never fit into your world, and I do not intend to allow any prince, no matter how handsome or sincere, to break my heart."

Omar swallowed hard, his heart thudding painfully. "Ellie, I . . ."

"I know that you think you care for me, Omar, but you love your family so much. Think of the heartbreak to your parents and your darling little brothers and sisters! You could never . . . *I* could never do that to them! Besides, Madame would never hire you at the castle and insult your parents."

"Then I will get a position somewhere else—" He reached toward her, but she pushed his hands away and took a step back.

"You hardly know me, and you cannot destroy your own future for my sake." Her voice cracked, and he saw tears spill down her cheeks. Again he tried to speak, but she rushed on. "I care too much for you to let you ruin your life for a summer romance, Omar. You are the most wonderful man I have ever, ever known, and I want you to live the life you deserve." Her voice caught on a sob as she backed away from him. "Please forget me and move on."

Just as she opened her door, he stepped forward, holding out her pack. As she lowered her eyes and took it, he said, "Never, Ellie." He spoke quietly, but he knew she heard him. "There will never be anyone but you."

CHAPTER FOURTEEN

ORNING ARRIVED FAR TOO EARLY. ELLIE LAY IN bed, remembering everything, dreading the day ahead. A familiar sound greeted her ears: the squeak of cinder sprites. A moment passed before she remembered she hadn't trapped any sprites since the Gamekeeper's visit. Her eyes popped open, possibilities rushing through her mind. Yesterday's rain would have driven sprites all over the resort into cover; she was likely to receive a message, or several, from the castle at any time. But the sprites she heard were inside her cottage; she was sure of it.

And they sounded hungry.

She popped out of bed, dressed in a clean coverall, and slipped on her glass shoes and her gloves. There should be fresh kale and collard greens in her refrigerator, and the Gamekeeper had left a supply of empty cages. With spray bottle in hand, she slipped out of her bedroom and surveyed the small living area. Two sprites scampered into view, one chasing the other, oblivious to her presence. They were not much larger than her fist and quick on their little feet. One was solid red, the other white with black ears, nose, and feet, and their hair was long and straight, parted down the middle and flowing behind them. They looked like animated wigs but for their spiraled horns. In her three years of working with cinder sprites, Ellie had only ever seen one quite like them.

"Good morning, babies," she crooned, and filled the air with her soothing spray. The sprites paused, sniffing the air. Their squeaks softened in tone, and she heard little puffs of happiness. With any luck, she could trap them without ember incident.

She collected two cages and a handful of greens, then approached the tiny pair, who crouched in the open space between a chair and the small entry area, their little noses and ears twitching. "You might just be the cutest sprites I have ever seen," she told them, pouring on the charm. "You remind me of a sprite I met years ago." Slowly she set the cages on the floor then knelt. Their large black eyes studied her. Cinder sprites, though sentient, were generally not the brightest of creatures, but Ellie suspected she was being evaluated by sharp little minds.

Suddenly, so quickly that Ellie flinched, the white sprite trotted forward and hopped into her lap, puffing in a friendly manner. It nibbled at a zipper-pull on her pocket, then looked up into her face. Waves of trust and expectation flowed toward her. Ellie melted and offered the little creature a sprig of kale.

Soon she sat cross-legged on the floor with a sprite on each leg, both squeaking contentedly and munching on greens. She could only shake her head in wonder at their lack of fear. Had these two been living in her house unnoticed while she cared for the captive sprites? What had they lived on? She kept hay in a bin near the door, and pieces often dropped unnoticed while she cared for her little prisoners. Or the tiny intruders might have sneaked in and out through whatever entry point they had discovered.

Perhaps she could keep these two around for a time. The Gamekeeper allowed her to use discernment about allowing sprites demonstrating intelligence and restraint to remain in the castle gardens. Over the years she had released fewer than twenty, but those sprites never entered a human dwelling again, and she occasionally sighted them in the gardens.

Sprites were good company, and she always missed the cheery squeaks after the Gamekeeper visited and carried her captives away. She stroked the red one with the tip of her finger, and it made a little purring sound. These two fearless furballs were in no danger of going ember. "You two remind me very much of Starfire, the royal elder sprite. He had long hair like yours. Is he your father?"

The white sprite looked up, directly into her eyes, and gave a cheery squeak. Ellie grinned. That was a *yes*. Somehow these two seemed able to communicate emotion to her, much as the unicorn did. Cinder sprites were magical beings, but some of them, such as the elder sprite, had more control of their magic than others. Ellie shook her head. The complexities of the magic world seemed endless. Even her tutor Arabella still had much to learn.

Three years ago, cinder sprites had begun to appear on Faraway Castle property, triggering fear in resident pixies who believed (for no logical reason) that sprites threatened their food supply and homes. A group of pixies had begun threatening and frightening sprites in the attempt to eliminate them, for once a sprite burst into flame it would burn until it died.

That crisis had been the impetus for Ellie's promotion from ordinary worker to Controller of Magical Creatures, a position created for her by the Gamekeeper himself, much to the director's disgust. Ellie could trap most small magical beings who caused problems for the resort, but pixies had proven uniquely resistant to her magic. The elder sprite Starfire was the Gamekeeper's provision for pixie-protection for sprites and humans alike. Ellie had met the large, dignified sprite only once, but she knew he must still be around, for she seldom glimpsed pixies anymore, and cinder sprites were thriving. Ellie prided herself on her part in bringing these charming creatures back from the brink of self-extinction, for her herbal spray combined with her magic was the only known means of saving a sprite once it had "gone ember."

Before Ellie left for work, the two sprites were comfortably settled in a cage on her chest of drawers. With hay for bedding (and snacks) a generous supply of fresh greens, and a tube and a few balls for entertainment, they frolicked happily and even groomed Ellie's fingers with tiny pink tongues when she reached in to pet them.

Her prospects suddenly looked much brighter. She had a purpose in the world, a niche no royal princess could fill, no matter how blue her blood. Perspective was a wonderful thing.

Ellie worked that morning in the gardens with Rosa until a sprite event in a castle storeroom interrupted her tree-trimming. She handled everything with calm expertise and welcomed the emergency. She was professional. She was independent. She was impervious.

Until she carried a stack of cages through the side garden gate and heard running feet and a chorus of happy cries: "Ellie! Miss Ellie, did you catch more cinder sprites?"

Ellie stopped in her tracks, closed her eyes, and dammed up the rush of emotion threatening to flood her soul. Then she turned to smile at the Zeidan children. "I did! A whole family of them. One with tiny babies."

The children clustered around her, the two youngest hopping up and down on the service road, all talking at once. "Ellie, why haven't you been at the lake? Ellie, we miss you! Ellie, may I hold one? Ellie . . ."

She set down the cages and distributed hugs all around. Even Rafiq accepted one. "I have missed you too, my dears. Have you been at the beach today?"

"We were going there," he said, "but then Nanny had a headache and wanted a nap, so Omar said we could come and watch him play tennis—there's a playground right by the courts— so that's what we're doing now."

Ellie gave Rafiq a level look. "You are watching Omar play tennis?" She glanced around. "Some kind of new magical ability?"

Rafiq rolled his eyes. "The courts are right over

there. We saw you, and . . ." He shrugged, then picked up two sprite cages. "We came to help."

Explanation finished.

"Omar won't mind," Yasmine said. "He misses you too. He said so."

The children knew nothing about the unicorn expedition or its aftermath, of course. "Why don't you play with him?" Rita asked, hopping around Ellie's legs.

"Tennis, you mean? I have to work," Ellie said. "Tell you what. You all can help me carry the cinder sprites to my cottage, and then I'll walk you back to the tennis courts. And we'll hope Omar doesn't notice you're missing."

The children all agreed and rushed through the gate and the garden, then into the castle through a service door to collect cages. "We could help you in the garden too," Yasmine suggested.

"Thank you for the offer, but maybe another time," Ellie said, stacking two more cages atop the two already in Rafiq's arms. This sprite catch had been her largest yet: twelve, counting the litter of new babies. Once the children were loaded down with cages—Rita carrying only one but intensely proud and careful of her burden—they all trooped down the garden path, through the gate, along the service road, then through the strip of pines into the staff living quarters.

Seeing Ellie's home was a huge thrill for Rita and Karim, who tested every chair and searched her refrigerator. She allowed them to distribute carrots to the sprites, who perked up immediately. Three were still recovering from effects of going ember, but the others puffed and squeaked and munched. The children squeaked back to them, and a loud chorus soon filled the cottage.

Ellie offered the children apples, the only snack she had on hand, but while she was searching the refrigerator, two children disappeared. Rafiq and Karim accepted their apples and explained that the girls had gone exploring. Hearing cries of delight from her bedroom, Ellie knew she'd been found out.

Rita ran into the living room, her face glowing. "You have two sprites in your room—the cutest ever!"

Naturally, the boys needed to see for themselves, and Ellie was hard put to explain why these two sprites were not stacked with the others. The sprites put their paws up on the glass walls and greeted the children with happy squeaks. "May we hold them?" Yasmine inquired. "They don't look at all frightened."

Ellie couldn't argue. If the sprites didn't mind this much hopping and squealing from the children, they were unlikely to object to being held. She told the children to sit in a circle on the floor, then set the two sprites in the round space. "You can offer them bites of your apples," she suggested. "I'm out of carrots."

The red baby climbed immediately into Karim's lap, to his delight. "What are their names?" he asked. "This one should be Sparky. He looks like fire even when he's not burning."

"She," Ellie corrected. "They are both girls. But Sparky is a fine name."

"We could spell it with an *i*," Yasmine suggested. She lured the white sprite into her lap with a chunk of apple. "And this one should be Frosti. She is so pretty!"

Rafiq and Rita soon demanded their turns, and the sisters Frosti and Sparki were shuffled about by small hands without a hint of distress, answering to their names within moments. Ellie could only watch and wonder. She sensed nothing but contentment and pleasure from the little creatures.

But soon she had to break up the party. "Your brother might be looking for you by now," she reminded them. "Better put Sparki and Frosti back into their cage."

Rafiq and Yasmine claimed that privilege, and soon the sprites dined on apple cores, puffing and chirping their delight.

"Goodbye, babies," said Rita, waving at them through the glass.

"Goodbye, Sparki and Frosti," the others chorused.

Ellie steered her companions outside, privately thinking they were harder to herd than wild cinder sprites. "I don't want to go back to the tennis courts," Rita whined. "It's boring there. Can't we stay with you, Ellie?"

"How about we hop there like cinder sprites?" Ellie suggested, hoping to avert a storm. Taking Rita and Karim each by the hand, she began to hop and skip forward. They both joined in, and Yasmine took Rita's other hand to make a chain. At first Rafiq abstained, walking apart from the group and looking scornful. But he could not bear to be left out for long, and soon grabbed Karim's hand and took over the lead. Soon they were all running and skipping—and Rita's feet sometimes left the ground for several paces.

"Slow down now," Ellie ordered, fearing someone would fall. They arrived at the playground still in a chain but back to walking and hopping in a more controlled manner.

"Will you swing with me, please, please, please?" Rita begged, tugging on Ellie's hand, her big dark eyes pleading. Karim joined in, and the double dose of cuteness overcame Ellie's defenses. She found herself swinging on the playground between Rita and Karim, and unable to avoid watching the tennis match on the courts opposite.

Naturally, Omar looked amazing in white tennis attire, as did his partner, an athletic girl Ellie didn't recognize. They played against Briar and the pretty daughter of a nobleman from up north somewhere. And Ellie squirmed and burned with envy. She was good at tennis. She could have returned a serve Omar's partner missed. She . . . was only tormenting herself.

"Watch this, Ellie!" Rafiq did a handstand and turned it into a back flip, landing perfectly.

"Wow! That's impressive," she said honestly. Rafiq was small for his age but nimble and strong. In height he was unlikely to catch up with Omar, who was tallest of the brothers so far. Maybe Karim would be tall like Omar someday . . .

Why did everything always come back to Omar? She could never forget him while socializing with his family. Did she even want to forget him?

"I need to get back to work now," she said, dragging her feet to slow the swing. Her glass shoes filled with sand.

While she paused to empty them, Yasmine said, "Hello Omar! We found Ellie!"

How did he get here so fast? Ellie wondered in frustration. The tennis game must have ended while she was feeling sorry for herself.

"So I see. I wondered where you'd run off to." Omar did not sound pleased.

"We got to feed baby cinder sprites," Rita told him, trying to slow her swing with legs that barely reached the ground. Omar caught it by the chains to keep her from falling. Ellie didn't dare look up.

"Hello, Ellie!" a cheery voice called.

She lifted her head to return Briar's greeting.

He strolled across the grass, sweaty yet dapper in his tennis whites. "Good morning, Your Highness," she said.

He shook his head, amused. "Please call me Briar. We're friends."

"All right, Briar," she said, unable to resist his casual charm. Omar stood at the swing beside her, brushing sand from Rita's hair. "Good morning, Omar," Ellie said quietly. If only they could establish an easy friendship! But could that even be possible when her heart reacted so strongly to his presence? Maybe time would ease the pain.

"Good morning. Thank you for bringing the children back." He spoke without looking at her. She had never before seen his face so devoid of expression.

"Ellie," said Briar, "do you have a moment to talk? I need to discuss something with you."

"I must report to the lake soon for my afternoon shift," she said. "After a bite of lunch."

"May I walk you to the castle?" he asked.

She nodded. "I'll need to stop by my cottage for my gear first." She hugged the protesting children goodbye and promised to see them again soon.

Omar stood by, obviously trying not to watch and failing. His palpable hurt tore at her heart, but what could she do?

Briar spun his tennis racket and said nothing as they walked away from the playground. Only when well out of earshot did he comment. "Now, that was awkward. I won't butt in on your business, but I do want you to know that you needn't dread romantic overtures from me. Aside from a fundamental barrier between us, romance is impossible for me because I am on a . . . a quest, of sorts. As in, I am more-or-less committed."

"More-or-less committed sounds enduring," she observed. Was Omar the "fundamental barrier," or did he refer to their unequal stations in life?

"Ye-e-es, well. Even if I were an eligible suitor, I would never jeopardize centuries of peace between Auvers and Khenifra."

Ellie looked up sharply. "What?"

At first glance his expression was grave, but those intense eyes held a wicked twinkle. "My charming country excels at producing wine and romance. Military power, not so much. Khenifra would annihilate us on the battlefield as easily as a certain prince trounced another prince on the tennis court. I might stand a chance one-on-one with sabers or pistols, but on the whole, I hold with peaceful international negotiations."

Ellie couldn't repress a smile. "You are incorrigible."

"So I am frequently informed." One side of his mouth curled upward. "I wish you and Omar nothing but joy," he said plainly. "He is a good man. One of the best I've ever met. Maybe even good enough for you."

Ellie stiffened. "What did you wish to ask me?" she said as they approached her cottage.

"Before I get into that—Have you seen Tor?"

"No, I've been crazy-busy today. Is he back?"

"They say he was here yesterday, but I haven't seen him. The director returned last night, but no word about what happened."

"It is very strange." Conversation paused while Ellie collected her lake gear. Maybe she should ask the Gamekeeper; he probably knew all about the siren situation.

When she emerged from her room, Briar was studying the sprite cages in her sitting room. "How do you bear the noise they make?"

"I like it," she admitted. "They're good company."

"If you say so." He followed her back outside into bright sunlight, and they headed for the castle. "I'll have to talk fast. Ellie, how long have you worked here at the Faraway Castle?"

"This is my seventh summer, why?" She disliked his slightly interrogating tone.

"And where did you live before you came here?"

Ellie spoke and walked quickly. "I lived with the burva Arabella. She is better known as the Mountain Witch, but she hates that name. Arabella is cranky and peculiar, but she seeks only to help people." She knew she sounded defensive but couldn't help it. "She's always telling me to be kind and considerate and to look out for the interests of others."

"And she trained you to use your magic abilities?"

Ellie nodded then reconsidered. "Well, mainly she taught me how to mix herbal balms and potions, such as I use with the cinder sprites and other small creatures."

"How long have you lived with her?

Ellie felt her defenses rising. "For a long time.

Why do you want to know all this?"

"Trust me, it is important in a good way. Do you know your parents, your family?"

She stopped in her tracks. "How is this your business, Your Highness?"

He winced. "Back to titles again? I apologize, Ellie, but time is growing short. Please tell me, do you remember anything about your life before you lived with the burva Arabella?"

She stared at him for a long moment. "No. I don't." His gaze held hers, and she suddenly felt panic rise in her throat, stopping her breath. Terror filled her mind—flashing glimpses of huge talons, feathers, whirling depths—then blackness.

When Ellie's awareness returned, she was seated at a picnic table on the lawn beside the lake. She lifted her head from her arms and met Briar's concerned gaze across the table. "How long was I out?" she whispered.

"About five minutes. We've attracted some attention, but I chased people off. Great way to start new rumors."

Ellie couldn't respond to his humor. "Now you know my secret."

"Not really. Either your memory has been

wiped or your brain has blocked out something frightening. Neither would be your fault, Ellie." He patted her hand. "I don't expect you to talk to me, but it might be a good idea to tell someone everything you do remember and see if the rest won't come back to you." He sat back on the bench. "Meanwhile, you might want to head to the lake before you're late for work. I'll bring you a sack lunch, all right?"

She nodded, feeling grateful and somehow relieved.

CHAPTER FIFTEEN

❧⟨❦⟩❧

FTER DINNER THAT EVENING, ELLIE VISITED THE unicorns at the maternity barn. The mother unicorn, whose name, Miria told her, was Ulrica, was genuinely pleased to see her. Ellie held a strange one-sided-yet-not conversation with Ulrica. Each time she spoke to the creature, Ellie understood her better. Whether this was the unicorn's magic or her own, she wasn't sure. Ulrica clearly asked if she was certain the Gamekeeper did not prey on unicorns and other magical creatures. Ellie, while stroking baby Ulfr's fluffy mane, assured his mother that the Gamekeeper kept cinder sprites, imps, and unicorns safe at his hidden home, along with other, stranger creatures. For so she had heard from reliable sources.

Not until she was walking home did doubt begin to plague her mind. She had never seen this reserve for magical beasts. Was it real? Or . . . what if all this time she had been sending innocent creatures to feed a monster's appetite? But then, the elder sprite had trusted him, and the dwarfs and brownies did as well. These misgivings only ever troubled her when he was not around.

And then, to top off this troubling day, a shadowy figure waited outside her cottage door. "Who is there?" she asked sharply, sensing waves of animosity and a hint of magic.

"Where have you been?" a voice inquired, frightening in its way but a relief nonetheless.

"Good evening, Madame Genevieve. Welcome back. I assume you must know about the unicorns," Ellie said quietly. "I was visiting them."

After a pause, the director said bluntly, "You are aware that staff members may not attend resort dances."

"I am well aware, Madame. Is . . . is anything

wrong?"

"Many things are wrong," the woman snapped. "Do not add to the injustice and chaos by presuming on the fleeting interest of a foolish young prince. Remember your place."

She walked past Ellie toward the castle, a stiffly upright and strangely pathetic figure.

Ellie unlocked her door with a wave of her hand, closed it behind her, and leaned against it, breathing hard to repress fear, anger, and intense sorrow. Hearing welcoming squeaks from her bedroom, she hurried there and spent the next hour seated on her bed, watching greens disappear into puckered little mouths and enjoying the company of two furry and uncomplicated companions.

❧

Out on the lake again the next afternoon, Ellie sent her scooter bumping over choppy waves, relishing the cleansing wind and cold spray in her face. Ahead and to her right, she glimpsed spiny loops above the surface. Grinning, she slowed and shouted, "Ahoy there, my serpentine friend. Are you racing with me?"

A familiar weedy head appeared, showing its array of dagger teeth. The serpent made a strange sound, rather like a croupy cough, and its head, followed by yards of thick body, rose high above the waves then arced toward Ellie, passing over her head then down into the lake. Water poured over her as the serpent's entire length passed overhead, but she merely laughed and turned in a small circle within the arch, making her own whirlpool.

"Showoff," she shouted.

As the last of the serpent disappeared, the end of its tail wagged briefly. Ellie waved back, suspecting the monster watched her from underwater. Then she drove on. Who would have imagined that such a nightmare-looking creature would enjoy playing games?

A short time later she recognized Omar's friend Tor standing alone on the shore, apparently watching a family of ducks. She let her scooter drift in close and called, "Hello, Lord Magnussen. Are you feeling well?"

She saw her reflection in his sunglasses. His face was expressionless.

"Why would I not feel well? Do I know you?"

Ellie sensed a tangle of frustration and animosity in the man, though his emotions seemed general, not aimed at her.

There was no reason not to tell him. "I'm the lifeguard who pulled you off the island the other day," she said. She did back her scooter off slightly. He was very tall and built like a swimmer. There was no sense in taking chances.

"I see." His tone was flat. "What was I doing there?" He sounded cynical.

Ellie spoke without thinking first. "You were standing in the lagoon, talking with a siren."

He didn't move, but she sensed a change. He was suddenly alert, focused, though still sarcastic. "I was talking with a siren? I thought sirens only lured men to ruin then spurned them."

He was some distance away from her, yet as she listened to his voice and studied his face, she sensed a spell on him of a kind she had never seen before. "Not that siren," Ellie said. "She seemed devastated when I took you away."

There was no magic in her voice, yet her words paralyzed the man. After a long silence, he turned back to the ducks and said no more.

Ellie drove away, wondering if she really knew

much about sirens. Or men.

At dinner that evening, she sat with her friends, but her thoughts were far away. Every time she'd glimpsed Omar in the past few days, he'd been in the company of a different girl, playing what seemed to Ellie like every sport or game the resort offered. The man was in perpetual motion from sunrise to sunset, and she was sure he had worked hard to avoid catching her eye.

"Ellie's not listening anymore," Savannah said with a sigh.

"She never does." Kerry Jo picked up her tray. "All she thinks about is her cutie-pie prince."

"Whatever." Jeralee stood up too. "Come watch the volleyball tournament with us, Ellie?"

"Not tonight," Ellie replied. "But thanks." The last thing she needed was to bump into Omar in the company of yet another hopeful princess. She ducked out of the cafeteria, took a back door out of the castle, and hurried to her cabin alone with tears streaming down her face. Laughter and voices drifted from the shore, where happy guests gathered to watch beach volleyball and enjoy bonfires.

Hours later, alone in bed with only two sleeping

sprites nearby for company, Ellie struggled to fall asleep. Even though the "cutie-pie prince" had been scrupulously following her orders, she punched her pillow in effigy then blamed it for keeping her awake.

∽❦∾

It was late morning Friday—the day before the Summer Ball. Ellie had just delivered additional lemonade for a children's birthday party going on at the beach and was cutting across the lawn near the lakeshore, when she heard someone call her name. "Ellie, wait!"

Glancing back, she saw Yasmine and Rafiq racing toward her. "Didn't you see us at the party? We waved, but you wouldn't look our way," Yasmine said, panting as she wrapped Ellie in a damp, sandy hug.

"I'm sorry, I was thinking of other things," Ellie admitted. Guessing the Zeidan children would be at the party, she had tried to sneak in and out without being seen. The last thing she needed just then was more guilt about Omar. She already felt tears pressing at the backs of her eyes. One little nudge could open the floodgates.

"Omar is really sad," Yasmine told her. "I asked him why, but he wouldn't say. Would you talk to him, Ellie? He always seems happy when he is with you."

"The happiest ever," Rafiq added rather aggressively. He stood apart, arms folded across his chest.

Ellie swallowed hard. "I'm sorry about your brother, but I don't think I could cheer him up. He needs to find his own happiness. Besides, I've glimpsed him a few times these past few days, and he looked happy to me." Heartbreakingly so, in fact.

"You don't see him when no one's around," Rafiq said, almost growling. "He pretends to have fun when he's with people. When he thinks no one's looking, he stops faking."

Yasmine added, "Sometimes his eyes are all red, and he hardly talks to us anymore."

"Is he drinking?" Ellie asked in concern.

Rafiq gave her a scornful glare. "Omar? Duh! He is *crying,* Ellie. Because *you* don't talk to him anymore."

Feeling thoroughly chastised, Ellie apologized. "You don't understand. I don't want to hurt him, but . . . It's an impossible situation."

"Because our parents won't let him marry you," Rafiq said. "I'm not stupid. I know what's been going on. But just yesterday Omar told me he won't marry anyone else." He grabbed Yasmine by the hand. "C'mon. She doesn't care."

Yasmine looked back over her shoulder as Rafiq dragged her away. Her sorrowful, accusing eyes haunted Ellie throughout the day. A deep loneliness weighted her heart. The more she was around laughing, chattering people, the lonelier she felt.

True to his word, the Gamekeeper sent her a message that afternoon: He would arrive early in the morning to collect the sprites, and the unicorns as well if the mother wished to see the reserve.

Ellie immediately walked to the maternity barn and found Ulrica waiting for her. The unicorn sent waves of polite welcome and glowed brightly in the dim barn. Ellie would have loved to touch the beautiful creature but knew such liberties would be inappropriate.

As yet, Ulfr cared nothing for his dignity. He bleated and capered around the stall then butted his stubby horn into Ellie's leg and looked up at her with liquid-dark eyes. She petted him for as long as he would endure, and when he scampered off again, she turned to his mother. "The Gamekeeper will arrive early tomorrow. Do you wish to travel over the mountain pass to see the reserve?"

Ulrica answered in her wordless language that she was willing to go if Ellie came with them.

Ellie nodded. "I will come." Being far away on the day of the Summer Ball sounded ideal.

Her next stop was the director's office. The door was ajar, so she knocked then peered in. Madame looked up from her desk, and her already hard expression turned to slate. "What is it? I am busy."

"I need to inform you that tomorrow morning I will travel with the unicorns to the Gamekeeper's reserve. Ulrica has agreed to go as long as I go with them, and the Gamekeeper has given me permission."

Madame's green eyes seethed with scorn. "If you are foolish enough to go there, I will not stop you."

"Thank you" hardly seemed appropriate, but it

was the only response Ellie could produce.

As she withdrew, the director added, "You are wise, no doubt, to be far away when the Khenifran prince's betrothal is announced."

The Gamekeeper arrived before dawn. Ellie heard the wagon arrive on the service road and hurried to open her door. For some reason, today when the Gamekeeper's indistinct figure appeared from the darkness, a shiver ran down her spine. To conceal her reaction, she spoke with forced cheerfulness. "The sprite cages are here by the door. I'll help you load them before I bring out my things."

"You are coming?" The deep voice sounded surprised.

"Oh. Yes. I forgot to send you a message, didn't I?" Ellie's uneasiness increased. "I remembered to tell Madame but not you. I'm so sorry! Ulrica said she and Ulfr would go to the refuge if I came too. Do you . . . May I still come along?"

"You may." He stood there on her walkway, and she sensed that he was tentatively pleased. His uncertainty increased her courage. A little.

Ellie picked up a few cages and stepped outside. "I'll wait to load them until you show me where they go." She bravely walked past him and approached the wagon. It was hitched to strange creatures she could neither name nor fully perceive, creatures that seemed to gaze at her with luminous yellow eyes. Thinking back, she could not recall ever noticing any creatures hitched to the Gamekeeper's wagon. Yet always she had known it was a wagon, not a car or truck.

Not until the sprites in the cages she held began to crackle did Ellie realize she was shaking. Immediately she took a deep breath and spoke soothingly. "The Gamekeeper is good to all creatures, little ones. You needn't be afraid. I am traveling with you this time, and once we arrive, you will meet many more sprites and live in comfort for always."

The sprites yawned and squeaked sleepily. For once, her comforting words had calmed her own heart as well, and by the time the Gamekeeper approached she was able to speak to him normally.

"You have two sprites in a back room," he said. "Are they coming or staying?"

"They're coming with me," Ellie said. "I'll bring them."

Somehow, having those two little sprites along for the ride was a comforting idea. Their single cage was easy to carry, so Ellie picked up her backpack on her way out the door. Sparki and Frosti squeaked questions as she walked back to the vehicle. "We're going for a ride, little ones," she said softly, "to visit friends. And if you like it there, you can stay."

As she approached the wagon, her feet stopped moving. Sprite cages filled its bed, though she had no memory of the Gamekeeper carrying or loading any. She could not recall loading the first two she'd carried out. And now Frosti and Sparki peered at her from their cage directly behind the seat, next to her backpack. Her hands were empty.

So . . . the Gamekeeper truly did not enter her house when he collected sprite cages. Somehow this evidence of his truthfulness and respect for her privacy gave her courage to climb up on the seat beside him for the short ride to the stables. Again, he seemed mildly pleased but made no attempt to engage her in conversation.

Ellie tried not to notice the shadowy creatures pulling the van, and she almost succeeded. Part of her thought she might wake up any minute now and laugh at the bizarre dream she'd been having.

When they arrived at the stables, the Gamekeeper climbed down and walked to the back of the wagon . . . only now it was a van. Sprite cages filled a flatbed area behind the seat, but the rest of the vehicle was enclosed. The Gamekeeper opened the van, lowered its ramp, and instructed Ellie how to close it once the unicorns were inside. She followed his instructions, now nearly certain she was dreaming this entire adventure. Everything about it felt surreal.

"I will keep my distance from the unicorns until Ulrica is used to the idea of me," the Gamekeeper said humbly. "Once we are at the reserve, the other unicorns will ease her remaining fears."

So Ellie entered the maternity barn alone. Miria and Howurl greeted her at the door, their mournful faces even longer than usual. "The unicorns are ready to go," Miria said, "but how we shall miss them!"

Even Howurl mumbled something about

sadness and lonely. Ellie smiled, sensing his genuine affection for the lovely creatures. The brownies seemed real enough, and the stable smells were familiar and comforting. Maybe she was awake, after all?

The stall door was wide open, yet Ulrica and Ulfr waited at its threshold, their bodies and horns gleaming like starlight. Ulrica's glow dimmed briefly as she asked where the Gamekeeper was.

"He said he will keep his distance until you are used to him," Ellie explained. "I think he will allow the other unicorns to convince you of his goodness."

Ulrica bobbed her head up and down, waving that sharp horn about like a sword. Ellie clearly understood that Ulrica did not fear for herself, only for Ulfr. "I believe the Gamekeeper understands your feelings as well as I do," Ellie told the devoted mother.

She stood aside as Miria and Howurl made their farewells to the unicorns, speaking in a language she couldn't find words to describe. Then she led the unicorns to the van and explained how it would close up around them, leaving space above the ramp for air to flow. "You will be able to see the stars as we travel."

Ulrica paused, gazing toward the front of the vehicle, then led her son up the ramp and settled down on the bed of fresh straw in the spacious interior. She told Ellie that the pookas assured her of the Gamekeeper's goodness, so Ellie should not worry. Ulfr obediently lay down beside his mother, but his wide eyes sparkled with excitement.

Pookas, Ellie thought. Pookas pulled the van. How very strange. Still moving in this dream-world of reality, she climbed up on the wagon seat and found the Gamekeeper already there. He seemed nearly as shadowy as the pookas.

Ellie reached back with one hand to touch the sprite cages and took comfort from a duet of quiet squeaks and puffs. Lately it seemed that instead of her giving comfort to cinder sprites, they more often soothed her.

"They often soothe me as well," the Gamekeeper said, though she had not spoken a word. "I hope you may enjoy this trip, Miss Calmer. You will come to no harm and may, perhaps, find the help you need."

Ellie settled back on the bench, ready to begin.

Only to realize that the wagon-van was already moving along a mountain trail. She hadn't noticed when it started moving, let alone when it left Faraway Castle behind. A thrilling blend of fear and excitement swept over her at the prospect of traveling over the mountain pass in the company of this strange, mysterious being. More accurately, in the company of several strange, mysterious beings. Anyone would prefer such an adventure to a silly dance. Firmly she told herself that she didn't want to go to the Summer Ball anyway.

Only to realize with horror that she had spoken the words out loud.

CHAPTER SIXTEEN

URING THE AWKWARD PAUSE FOLLOWING HER declaration, Ellie sensed sympathy and hesitance from her companion. At last he spoke: "We have a long journey ahead, Miss Calmer. Perhaps voicing your frustrations and experiences will help you to better understand them. I would be honored to listen."

And somehow Ellie found herself pouring out everything, from her longtime crush on Prince Omar and the lemonade disaster to the cinder sprites in his bedroom and the past few days of separation and hurt. She even told about Prince Briar and her frightening and inexplicable reaction to his questions. No detail remained unspoken; never before had Ellie encountered such deep empathy and interest.

When her tale ended, she sensed that the Gamekeeper was pondering her tale, but she could not guess which aspect of it caught his attention. He spoke slowly, choosing each word with care. "Your magical gifts have expanded significantly in the past week, I believe."

Ellie considered this idea and realized he spoke the truth. "I think you're right, but I don't know how or why this is so."

"Although I believe contact with the lake serpent and sirens contributed to your growth, most likely your interactions with the unicorn are the main catalyst. The desire to communicate with Ulrica motivated you to exercise and expand your inherent abilities. I wonder if you might use this newly discovered insight to explore your own memory and emotions. Tell me what you know about your childhood, about whatever brought you to Arabella."

"Do you know her?" Ellie asked in surprise.

"We have met." She could sense no emotion in his voice or manner.

"I was a child when I came to her house," she began. "Arabella told me I simply appeared one day on her doorstep. I was traumatized, she believed, and fear had erased or blocked out memory of my entire past. She quickly discovered I had magical ability so trained me extensively in herb lore and the basic use of my voice to soothe creatures. Always she emphasized the importance of kindness, of using my limited powers for the good of other creatures."

"Why do you describe your powers as limited?"

"Many creatures are able to block them."

"Your powers are greater than you believe them to be," the Gamekeeper responded in a rumbling tone. Ellie blinked in surprise. Could it be *amusement* she heard in his voice?

"You were not left on Arabella's doorstep by chance or error," he continued. "The flashback you experienced yesterday revealed important facts." He paused, then said, "I know someone who might shed light on your past. But we have other things to accomplish first today."

As soon as the Gamekeeper spoke, the van passed through huge iron gates set in a stone wall. Ellie sat forward and gaped, aware at last of her surroundings. The wheels of the van seemed to skim the ground rather than roll, for it traveled with impossible speed and smoothness. Wild forestland swept past, then broad green meadows, then hillsides, lakes, and chattering streams. Ahead, perched on the side of the mountain, with the sweeps of meadow and forest before it and a cliff at its back, she saw a magnificent castle. Not a fortress of war or practical manor house, but a fantastical golden palace of spires and pinnacles and balconies and sparkling windows, all drawing closer at a dizzying rate.

The van swept around a circular drive and stopped smoothly before a broad stone staircase leading to tall double doors. Ellie gripped the bench seat with both hands and stared, still open-mouthed, as the doors opened wide . . . and no one emerged.

"If you will help release the unicorns, my servants will then care for your needs and wishes. I shall join you for luncheon in a few hours." The Gamekeeper offered her a huge gloved hand, and Ellie allowed him to help her down. He then swept her an elegant bow and stepped out of sight. Where and how, she could not tell. Just as she could not perceive the pookas, though evidence of their existence was undeniable, so she could not understand how the Gamekeeper could walk away invisibly.

But she had a job to do. Giving her head a little shake, she took control of her rubbery legs and walked to the rear of the van. Quickly she lowered the ramp and saw the unicorns standing ready.

Ulrica sucked in deep draughts of clear mountain air, and Ellie clearly heard the unicorn's heart sing for joy: This is our true home! Ulfr tried to hide behind his mother's legs, but curiosity compelled him to stare out at this enormous new world. Soon his little legs straightened, and his head lifted high, nostrils quivering.

Ulrica filled her lungs and gave a bugling call, clearer than the purest notes ever produced by a trumpet. And Ellie heard a veritable concert in response. She turned to behold a company of unicorns ascending the slope of meadow, their bodies glistening in the sunlight, nearly too bright for Ellie's eyes to bear. Ulrica and Ulfr trotted forward to meet their kin, and cries of rejoicing and reunion both silent and audible filled Ellie's heart with joy. For Ulrica's mate was there, a tall unicorn with a blue beard and glistening horn. He greeted his wife and son with joy and pride that sent tears streaming over Ellie's cheeks.

Until she noticed, with some annoyance, that fingers were plucking at her sleeves. The servants! Curiosity turned her around to see . . . nothing. Sprite cages wafted across the courtyard, and her backpack floated up the stairs and through the open doorway.

She heaved a little sigh. Invisible and inaudible, no doubt. But perhaps she could sense their thoughts or emotions if she focused hard enough. Obeying the direction of those plucking hands, she followed her pack up the steps and into a hall so resplendent with gold, carvings, moldings, and works of art that her mind simply blended it all into one word: magnificent. The escort servants—she thought there were two, both female—led her through equally magnificent hallways and drawing rooms on the way to a much smaller yet comfortably luxurious suite of rooms, including a private bath with running water, hot and cold, and a huge canopied bed.

Bemused and tired, Ellie submitted to her invisible helpers with gratitude and fascination, even allowing them to undress and bathe her, wash and arrange her hair, and dress her in lace-and-silk undergarments and a lavender-scented morning gown in the style of a previous century. She spoke to them occasionally but mostly soaked in the luxury of being pampered like a princess. What manner of creature was the Gamekeeper, she wondered, that he would dwell in such a castle?

But she was reluctant to explore possibilities lest they disturb her enjoyment of the moment. After all, he had done nothing to deserve distrust and everything to earn her respect. She slept on the bed for what seemed like hours but could not have been long, for the clock on the mantel chimed noon just as the door opened and her servants returned.

Ellie slipped on her glass shoes, which seemed clunky with her frilly gown, and followed her attendants downstairs to a hall in which a great table had been set for luncheon. The Gamekeeper waited for her, standing behind a chair at the table's far end. "You may choose any seat," he said quietly. Since no other guests were in view, Ellie walked along the table and pulled out a chair a few settings away from him. She no longer feared her supervisor, yet she was more comfortable with some space between them.

Ellie did justice to the meal, talking all the while about her room and the servants and her impressions of the castle. The Gamekeeper asked leading questions, and she found herself telling more about her life at Faraway Castle, including her questions about Rosa's secret ways, the director's attitudes, and Briar's confusing behavior. Afterward she could not recall whether the Gamekeeper had eaten anything.

Strange, how she felt so alive yet so immersed in unreality!

When she laid her fork on her plate and declared herself stuffed, the Gamekeeper said in his quiet way, "Would you like to see where your cinder sprites live?"

"Yes, very much!" A servant pulled out her chair as she rose, and her host politely offered his arm. She hesitated only an instant before laying her hand on his sleeve. "Thank you." He now wore a cloak of deep blue velvet edged in ermine, and his large feet were clad in equally fine boots.

They passed through an outer door into the

fresh summer day, then across a courtyard, past an ornate fountain, and into an outbuilding. "The sprites have indoor shelter as well as open land, but their habitat is entirely fenced to keep out predators. They do not multiply as rapidly as non-magical beasts of their size do, since they are sentient and mate for life. Most females birth only one or two litters."

Ellie gazed in wonder at the low yet extensive shelters inhabited by dozens, even hundreds, of chirping, puffing, squeaking sprites. "Did all of these sprites come from Faraway Castle?"

"Most of them. A few traveled here and requested to be allowed in to join their families."

"Do any ever wish to leave?"

"Not so far. Perhaps, in time, a new generation will wish to see more of the world. I will not keep them captive."

Several of the little creatures looked familiar to Ellie, including the mother and family she had captured in Omar's room. With them she saw a large male who'd arrived with them that day. The family was happily united.

"All structures are flame-proof," the Gamekeeper continued, "and their enclosure is well watered in all seasons. Occasionally one will become angry or panic and burst into flame, but their relative safety and commodious accommodations limit such events."

"They seem happy," Ellie said, sensing waves of tiny emotion throughout the enclosure. "I wonder if any of them remember me."

"Two of them do." The Gamekeeper pointed with a long finger (claw?) at the ground near her feet. Two cinder sprites sat nearly upright, their front paws pressed against the tempered-glass wall of their enclosure. Their working mouths, bobbing horns, and twitching ears indicated squeaks that had been lost in the clamor of the busy colony. Only now did Ellie distinguish their little voices.

"Sparki and Frosti," she cried in delight, and knelt to touch the glass opposite their paws. "My special babies." Two other sprites approached, one solid black with messy-looking fur and horns like spirals of obsidian, the other solid brown with a whorl of white on his forehead, sleek fur, and bronze-colored horns. They strutted and posed, much like teenaged boys, and her two girls evidently liked them. Ellie looked up at the

Gamekeeper in surprise. "The girls are so young! Do they have boyfriends already? After one morning?"

She sensed his amusement. "They are old enough to choose mates. These two are not only the youngest daughters of Royal Elder Sprite Starfire and his mate, Dusk, but also enjoy the distinction of being named. Cinder sprites do not name themselves. It sets them apart. Yet these two males are confident enough to enjoy having celebrity mates."

Ellie boggled. "I had no idea!" She looked back over the colony in wonder. Those little creatures scurrying here and there, eating, chirping, fighting, playing—they shared community and had social structures. "I have so much to learn about magic beasts!"

"Time is passing in your world, however, and we have much to do." He again offered his arm, and Ellie, after blowing kisses to her sprite friends, again accepted his escort.

This time he paused in an open area. "I intend to transport us by magic to the home of a creature that may be able to shed light on certain events in your past. You need not fear; I will allow no harm to come to you. Do not let go of my arm."

Before Ellie could think to ask a question, he stretched out his free arm and seemed to push against the air. They stepped forward as if through a doorway, and everything went dark. It felt dry and cold and infinitely black. Without realizing, she lowered her chin and closed her eyes. Then she felt a jolt, as if she'd been jerked sideways, and a fresh, cold breeze struck her face.

"We're here," the Gamekeeper said. "Vlad should arrive shortly. I sent a message."

When Ellie hesitantly opened her eyes, her chin still tucked, the first thing she saw was a terrible emptiness before her feet, as if the ground had been cut off and dropped away. She shrieked, squeezed her eyes shut again, clung to the Gamekeeper's arm, and moaned, "Where have you taken us?"

CHAPTER SEVENTEEN

'M TERRIFIED OF HEIGHTS!" ELLIE SCARCELY recognized that shrill voice as hers.

The Gamekeeper stepped away from the precipice, bringing Ellie with him. "I apologize. I hadn't thought how the altitude might affect you. Come. I brought us here to the entrance rather than invade the family's privacy, but we can move further into the cave." As they turned, she glanced back and realized they stood at the entrance of a cave near the top of a sheer mountain surrounded by other peaks. Despite the glaciers all around and a brisk wind, she did not feel cold, yet terror sent tremors through her body and her teeth chattered.

At the Gamekeeper's urging, her feet moved even as her brain felt immobile. Not until solid walls surrounded her and the cave opening was a bright spot in her peripheral vision did she begin to relax.

"What is this place? It smells strange."

"We are at the home of a magical creature who may be able to shed light on your history," the Gamekeeper replied. He spoke quietly, yet his voice always made her soul shiver. "I sent a message and expect him to arrive shortly. I will allow no harm to come to you, Miss Calmer." He sounded genuinely regretful.

But then she heard a cry that turned her blood to ice. Slowly she looked up and saw her nightmare alight at the cave's entrance. Burning yellow eyes, feathers, talons reaching to grab her, an open beak . . . Ellie screamed . . .

She saw spinning mountain peaks beneath her, felt the rush of wind that blocked all other sound, including her own screams. Then something grasped her arms, jerking her body forward and up instead of down. Her head snapped back, and she stared up at the underside of a strange birdlike creature.

"You are safe, Ellie. He will not harm you." The voice seemed to speak into her thoughts, into her memory.

Ellie opened her eyes but saw only the Gamekeeper's hooded profile. She still stood upright, clinging to his arm. Briefly she considered the fact that she was at the mercy of not one but two monsters. Yet his presence was comforting after all.

For he stood between her and the creature now silhouetted against the cave's entrance: an enormous griffin.

Cruel yellow eyes stared at her, a huge beak snapped in irritation, and long talons clicked on the stone floor as it approached, folding its wings. "Why have you come?" It spoke clearly, its tone regal and resentful.

"Greetings, Vlad."

The griffin lowered its head in response. "Your Eminence."

Only then did the Gamekeeper answer, "I wish to know if you once captured a human girl-child and left it at Arabella's door."

The creature's golden neck feathers ruffled.

"What if I did?"

"The child survived. I merely wish to know your side of the story."

The griffin sat down, and the tufted tip of its tail twitched. "I didn't know the foolish thing was magical until it persuaded me to let it go! Fortunately, I dropped it from high altitude and was able to catch it before it hit the rocks. I apologized and took it to Arabella because she was nearby."

"Where did you first find the child?"

"In a high meadow near Grim's Peak. The humans looked ordinary enough. It was an honest mistake." The griffin studied Ellie briefly. "You were that child," it said. "I recognize your magic. It is stronger now. And weaker. You don't trust it."

"Wh-why did you take me?" Ellie asked.

The griffin's ears flattened against his feathered head. "Human girls make good servants. In my homeland, every nesting couple keeps one in the den to clean and to watch over the young." He snarled a strange combination of an eagle's scream and a lion's roar. "It's not as if we kill and eat them."

Ellie felt a weight lift from her heart. "I am glad

to know that you didn't intend to kill me," she said.

Vlad's tail lashed from side to side. "Kill you? I went to the trouble of catching you again after you blasted me with magic and made me drop you, even though I knew I could not take you home with me. And I left you with Arabella, the best place for any human child that could force me to drop it."

"Why did you not explain to Arabella?"

Vlad preened a few chest feathers. "I figured you would tell her. I had to go in search of a more suitable candidate. My mate was near her time." His feathered shoulders shrugged.

"I hope your family is well," Ellie said.

The griffin shrugged. "That clutch is grown now and spread across the continent, but they all four send us messages occasionally."

"What became of the replacement servant girl?" Ellie asked in some concern.

"She was free to go once our brood had flown. Being a sturdy creature, she walked down the mountain with a satchel full of gold and found her way home, none the worse and much the richer for the experience."

Ellie decided not to comment on the girl's lost months with her family and the worry caused to all concerned. Instead, she looked at the Gamekeeper. "Did you know about the slave girl?"

"I did not."

The griffin's neck feathers fluffed out. "Human girls always tend young griffins. It is a time-honored tradition and beneficial to all concerned. We pay generously."

"I should defend the tradition myself if only the girls chose to accept the position," Ellie said. "To steal them away is inexcusable. Why not ask for volunteers? I should think the Gamekeeper could help you locate promising candidates."

Vlad growled softly. "It is our business, not his. Bad enough that he owns a key to our home."

"You chose the den with full knowledge that it lay partly inside my domain," the Gamekeeper said in his quiet yet emphatic way, and the griffin lowered himself into a crouch.

"It is the Gamekeeper's business to protect magical creatures from humans and humans from magical creatures," Ellie said in her best persuasive tone.

"Only those within his borders. But I'll think

on it. Not because you're using your magic on me, mind you, human!"

"My name is Ellie," she said. "Can you tell me anything about my family?"

Vlad's yellow eyes fixed on her. "I seem to recall several humans standing near a vehicle, a few seated on the ground on a piece of cloth, and smaller ones running about. I snatched the small female." He looked Ellie up and down. "You are large now."

"That was eleven years ago," Ellie said sadly. "And I remember nothing about my family." Tears burned the back of her eyes, but she refused to give in to a wave of sorrow.

For the first time, the griffin looked slightly regretful. "I was unaware that humans cared about family, there are so many swarming about. But perhaps they can recognize differences among themselves."

"We do." Ellie swallowed hard before adding in a slightly choked voice, "And we love our families very much."

"Then I hope you find yours," Vlad said in a magnanimous tone. He gave the Gamekeeper a look. "Will you please leave now? I am already late. Mirka would be furious to learn that you have been inside our cave."

"We shall leave," the Gamekeeper said. "Thank you for your time, and best wishes to you and Mirka."

"Goodbye, Vlad," Ellie said, trying to sound gracious. "Thank you for taking me to Arabella."

"You are welcome," the griffin said in an almost genial tone. "Farewell, enchanters."

When they turned, Ellie again felt the tug, and stepped with the Gamekeeper into the meadow near the cinder-sprite enclosure. Curious, she turned around in time to see a vertical black rectangle narrow into a line then disappear, as if an invisible door into darkness had closed.

"This is all so very strange," she said, blinking hard. "I am not sure I will remember it fully once I leave here."

"You will remember everything that matters," the Gamekeeper said, and led her back down the slope. "We have another important errand today."

"Very well." Ellie was unable to keep her voice from quivering.

"This one will not frighten you." He sounded slightly amused.

As they returned to the castle, Ellie pondered that strange meeting and realized the most important fact she had learned. "I have a family. The griffin stole me from my family. I thought I was abandoned, but all this time they may have been looking for me, missing me!" She looked up at the Gamekeeper's hooded head. "Why couldn't they find me? Did the griffin carry me so very far away?"

"Grim's Peak is not far from here," her strange companion answered quietly. "Arabella is difficult to find unless she wishes to be found."

They entered the castle through the great outer doors and climbed the staircase, and climbed the staircase, turning left at the landing. "Wait!" Ellie stopped short on a stair. "This staircase! It reminds me of something." Her heart pounded. "I remember dancing on the floor of a large house with a staircase that went straight up toward a wall with a crest on it, then branched off toward the two sides, leading to long open galleries filled with paintings and artwork." She ran her hand over the smooth railing and stared at it without seeing. "I was a very good dancer!" she added in some surprise. "I never knew I could dance. Perhaps I was a performer?"

"Do you recall any faces or voices?"

She racked her brain, but it stubbornly went blank. "No. But now I really want to try dancing again!" She thought of the Summer Ball with a twinge of regret.

"I believe you should."

Without another word, the Gamekeeper continued up the stairs and led Ellie into a suite of rooms far finer than her guestroom. There he opened an enormous wardrobe to reveal gowns of every imaginable color and style, layer upon layer of them.

Ellie realized vaguely that there were too many gowns for the size of the wardrobe but set aside that thought for another time. For the Gamekeeper drew out a violet gown made of some shimmery substance she could not identify and said, "You may wear this to the Summer Ball, if you so choose." He hung the gown on the wardrobe door, then handed Ellie a matching creation of feathers and sparkling stones—an elaborate feathered domino.

She stared at the mask, then at the gown, then at the Gamekeeper. "But how can I attend the ball? Even with a gown, I am only a staff member, not a guest."

"Not one of Faraway Castle's workers is 'only' a staff member, Miss Calmer. You are a gifted enchantress in the truest sense of the word, you are a woman who understands how to love unselfishly, and you are a lady from your heart outward. No amount of royal blood could make you worthier to attend this ball than you already are. Your prince Omar understands this as few people do."

Ellie gaped in awe at these declarations spoken in a regal voice so different from the Gamekeeper's usual quiet tones. "But Omar . . . My position . . ."

"Neither you nor the prince will suffer from your attendance at this ball. Take courage, Miss Calmer. Do this for Omar's sake."

Ellie felt courage rise in her breast, and with a lift of her chin and a squaring of her shoulders, she stated, "I shall attend the Summer Ball, and I shall dance with Prince Omar!"

Afterward she could never clearly recall the period immediately following her declaration, but she knew that the Gamekeeper had vanished again. His servants dressed her in the fabulous gown and domino, along with glittering jewelry and white gloves. The one thing she did not allow was an ornate hairstyle; she felt far more comfortable in her usual simple ponytail, dressed up with a few flowers.

After a wondering stare at her reflection in a tall mirror—even with the ponytail she looked like a stranger—Ellie walked down the castle's front steps to behold a wondrous golden coach hitched to six unicorns, which nodded graciously to her and communicated that they had volunteered for the honor of drawing it and were delighted to be chosen. The Gamekeeper had designed the coach for the occasion, she learned.

"Out of a pumpkin," an actual voice said, interrupting the unicorns. "It was the shape he needed and near at hand. Try not to let your gown touch the inner walls or it might stain." Ellie felt a chill down her spine at the laugh following this disclosure. One of the pookas, now in more-or-less human form, sat on the driver's seat with the reins in one distorted hand, his yellow eyes aglow, his large buck teeth gleaming in a wide grin.

"Indeed! How very . . . creative." Ellie tried to return the creature's disturbing smile and was profoundly relieved when the unicorn she recognized as Ulrica's mate spoke clearly into her mind: "Never fear, Ellie Calmer. We unicorns will deliver you directly to the ball no matter what tricks the pooka might attempt."

Hearing a muffled squeak, Ellie glanced at a coach lamp, then stared around in dismay. Inside each lamp glowed a flaming ball with bright red eyes. Had these cinder sprites been frightened or enraged to the point of going ember? The idea disturbed her deeply. But Ulrica's mate, Ucal, as he introduced himself, assured her: "The sprites are delighted to provide your lighting, my lady. Nothing but excitement fuels their glow, and they will not burn out. On this blessed day you are a great lady in the eyes of all magical creatures, for you rescued my wife and son."

Invisible hands opened the coach door, and Ellie stepped forward as if in a dream. Just as she lifted her skirts to climb inside, the Gamekeeper spoke at her elbow, giving her an inward jar. But she stepped back with composure and smiled, gradually processing his words: "I have one more gift for you, Miss Calmer."

He didn't seem to notice the slight pause

between his words and her glance downward at the object in his hand. Objects, for it was a pair of shoes. "Glass dancing slippers? Did you make those for me?"

"They are exactly like your work shoes in size and durability," he said quietly.

Ellie leaned against the coach doorway, pulled off her clunky work shoes, and slipped on the tempered-glass dancing shoes. Invisible hands picked up the old shoes and placed them in her pack, then stowed the pack in a bin behind the driver's seat, but Ellie scarcely noticed.

She paced back and forth beside the coach. "They are comfortable as well as beautiful." When she lifted her skirts to peer at her feet, the faceted-glass slippers sparkled. "Thank you for everything, my kind friend, and especially for the shoes. They even make my feet look small! Your magic never fails to amaze me."

The tears in her eyes made him seem more shadowy than ever. Nothing she could say or do would ever repay his generosity and goodness.

He spoke as if reading her thoughts, his voice quiet yet profoundly deep: "I ask only that you allow nothing to destroy your joy tonight, Miss

Calmer."

Ellie nodded, lips quivering, her heart too full even for a smile.

Then she climbed into the coach, waved out the window, and called, "Thank you, everyone!" then settled back on the cushioned seat. The interior walls of the coach were similar in hue to a squash, but she detected neither moisture nor vegetable scent, no matter what the pooka said.

The coach seemed to float over the road without a bump or jolt. Aside from the rush of wind and an occasional happy squeak or chortle from a sprite, the journey was uncannily quiet. By the time Ellie thought to peer out the windows, she saw nothing but trees flashing past, with occasional open views of mountainous terrain beneath a colorful sunset sky. Recalling that unicorns pulled the coach, Ellie put all worries about time out of her head and leaned back, resting her eyes. The feathered domino made it difficult to see much anyway.

What would Omar think when she entered the ballroom? Would he recognize her?

"We are nearly to the castle, my lady," the pooka called to her. "Where would you like to be dropped off? In the lake?"

She heard a chorus of protests from the unicorns, and Ucal's assurance rose above the rest. "Don't mind him. We have orders to deliver you to the door of Faraway Castle. Your friends Sparki and Frosti will direct us there."

"Thank you, all of you," Ellie said aloud. She hadn't recognized her sprite friends in their ember form.

The castle glittered with paper lanterns, spotlights, and tiny white lights strung around pillars, doors, and windows. Several fine automobiles and limousines waited in a queue, yet somehow there was room for Ellie's coach directly before the main doors. A liveried footman opened her coach door, pulled out the step, and offered his gloved hand. "My lady," he said politely.

Ellie restrained a smile, recognizing her old friend Ben Weatherby, one of the groundskeepers. She laid her gloved hand in his and stepped gracefully from the coach. His eyes widened at the sight of her, but he did not return her friendly smile. "My lady," he breathed in wonder.

Before he could escort her inside, she turned back to thank the magical creatures—only to realize with a start that a glamour now disguised them even from her eyes. Lightbulbs burned in the coach lamps, a man in a gray wig and sharp livery sat on the box (he winked at her), and six fine coach horses tossed their heads. But then two of the side lamps blinked, and one of the horses turned its head to look directly at her. She heard cinder sprites squeak and puff along with Ucal's gentle farewell: "Our love and blessing to you, Miss Cinder Ellie."

"I love you too," she whispered. The coachman lifted the reins, and the coach pulled away with a great clatter of horse hooves on the brick drive. It moved into the shadows and was gone.

Along with her backpack.

CHAPTER EIGHTEEN

THE INSIDE OF THE CASTLE WAS AS TRANSFORMED as its exterior, with lights twinkling everywhere. Ellie had often seen it decorated for dances and other special occasions, yet something about this night was different, and she didn't believe the difference was only in her perception. Perhaps she had brought magic with her from the Gamekeeper's house?

Older guests congregated in the large seating area in the lobby, most of them beautifully dressed and the ladies glittering with jewels. A few wore masks, but most didn't bother. A masquerade was for the young people. Small children and their hovering nannies dashed here and there, and staff members rushed about on errands. Ellie sensed curiosity and admiration from people she passed, and she wondered if they sensed the magic surrounding her as well.

Tonight she could do anything, be anything. And more than anything else, she wished to dance with Prince Omar of Khenifra and be seen by others as his equal, not in rank but in value. Omar was a good dancer, she knew, having watched him furtively over the years at many events. Not a particularly inspired dancer, but expertly trained and graceful. Ellie had always considered herself his opposite, inspired but not trained. Now she knew better, and the knowledge fueled her excitement and anticipation.

As she approached the ballroom, brownies darted past her feet. The guests could not see them and even overlooked the objects they carried, and the little creatures nimbly dodged feet and skirts without dropping a fork or a chocolate biscuit. Every one of them greeted Ellie by name, and not one seemed to notice her unusual appearance.

Sira, carrying a stack of dirty plates, paused to

address her, concern etched in her small brown forehead beneath a neat white cap. "Miss Ellie, Geraldo has sworn to steal a cake off the dessert table tonight, and he's persuaded the other hobgoblins to help him. You know they will end up dumping it on the floor and allow children to take the blame!"

Ellie couldn't help smiling. The hobgoblins' purpose in life seemed to include doubling the brownies' workload. Yet Sira worried only about trouble for the human children.

"I will try to keep an eye on him," she said. "Everything looks amazing, Sira. Please share my appreciation with the other brownies."

Sira merely nodded before trotting away. "Enjoy yourself, Miss Ellie." Her little voice trailed behind her.

"Thank you, Sira."

A few guests watched Ellie talk to the floor, their faces revealing doubt of her sanity, yet not one said a word. She beamed a general smile at the spectators then picked up her skirts and hurried toward the ballroom door. Music floated into the hall, a modern love song. The live bands always played a variety of dance tunes to satisfy guests of all ages and nations.

She paused in the doorway before entering. Often she had imagined entering this room as a guest, but never once had she believed her daydream could come true. Would it end in bliss or in nightmare?

Music, conversation, and laughter filled the air, along with delectable scents from the buffet tables. The floor, polished to a mirror shine, reflected the gleaming chandeliers and strings of lights, resembling a starlit lake. Couples floated over the dance floor, their attire ranging from elegant ballgowns, modern cocktail dresses, and tuxedos to historical or national costumes. Everyone on the dance floor wore a mask of some kind, as did most of those on the outskirts. Ellie identified a few people yet thought it strange how even the simplest mask could transform a friend into a mysterious stranger. But she could delve behind the masks if she tried . . .

The girl in green with strawberry-blonde curls had to be the Honorable Gillian, dancing with a young man with golden hair, who steered her effortlessly around the floor and made her look quite good. As they moved closer to Ellie, she recognized Prince Briar. He glanced her way, pale eyes glinting behind his mask. A rush of anticipation and affection flowed toward Ellie— then cut off as if a door had slammed in her face.

But he couldn't keep everything from her. The instant Ellie met his gaze, she knew he danced with Gillian only to keep her from causing trouble for Omar.

Poor girl. Prince Briar was a rogue. But then, Gillian herself was a shrew, and Ellie couldn't bring herself to like her.

However, she liked Briar, rogue though he was. Not in a romantic way, but with genuine regard. They had met only days before, yet just now he had recognized her instantly despite her mask and seemed to sense her emotions as clearly as she sensed his.

Her smile turned to a slight frown. How did he manage to shut her out? No one else could, not tonight.

Ellie eased her way further into the room and stood against the wall. This new power of hers could easily become unbearable if she didn't learn to control it. The emotions and thoughts wafting toward her from all sides were almost overwhelming: hints of yearning, envy, desire, amusement, delight, and sorrow.

Had her glimpses into Prince Briar's heart enhanced her gift? Or was it the unicorns, or the Gamekeeper? She struggled to block these random impressions and instead focused on individuals.

There was King Aryn at a table near the garden doors, playing cards with three nobles. He was content enough with his hand and his situation, relaxed and confident. Ellie had always liked the king's earnest face that reflected his inner man.

Queen Sofia sat amid other ladies and talked. The woman's smooth features and bright smile revealed little of the varied blend of emotions stirring within her. Love—there was so much love in Omar's mother. Touches of concern as well, but underlying faith and serenity prevented it from lining the queen's face.

The song ended, and several of the dancers walked off the dance floor and scattered. Others went in search of new partners or simply waited for the next song to begin. Ellie was working up courage to thread her way around the room in search of Omar when someone addressed her in a voice she instantly recognized: "Good evening, mysterious lady in violet. May I have the honor of your next dance?"

Silvery eyes gleamed at her from behind a plain black domino. Ellie grinned. "You may, sir." Prince Briar was an expert dancer. This should be fun.

He led her to the floor, and as soon as the lively music began and Briar twirled her into a backward dip, she could have laughed for joy. How had she lived without dancing all these years? Facing her and holding her hands, the scoundrel prince from Auvers led her in a series of intricate steps, and Ellie followed him with ease, as if they had practiced these moves together a thousand times, as if this moment had been selected from among her lost memories. He spun her, twirled her in a fancy lift, and she ended the swing dance in a back dip over his knee, her foot in its glass slipper twinkling high in the air. Panting and smiling in delight, Ellie heard applause all around and realized that the other dancers faced them in a wide circle. Several cried out, "Bravo! Bravo! That was amazing!"

As Briar pulled her upright, he laughed, his triumph matching hers. "I knew it," she gasped between pants. "I knew I could dance! How did you learn to dance so well?"

He gave her a sharp glance, and she didn't need magic to sense his disappointment. "I took lessons for many years." A pause. "And you?"

"I . . . I think I did too."

"You think? You don't know?"

Ellie stared into his eyes, feeling strangely as though she looked into a mirror. "Briar . . ."

Then his gaze moved past her. "Ah." He straightened his shoulders and cleared his throat, evidently repressing a smile. "Your dance, sir?"

"I hope so."

Ellie spun to face Omar. She could not read his expression through his mask but sensed waves of uncertainty and hurt. "Omar," she breathed, and his expression brightened, for in that one word she revealed her feelings for him.

"Dance with me?" His whisper was a plea.

Ellie laid her hand in his and waited for the music to start. Other couples joined them on the floor, but Ellie saw only Omar. He looked amazing in a tuxedo, its snowy collar and cravat bright against his dark skin; and his eyes glittered through the eye-holes of a simple domino. She did not expect him to dance as well as Briar, but it didn't matter. She was thrilled to dance with him no matter what!

Having no dance card, she had no idea what to expect, so when a trumpet played the first notes, she nearly laughed aloud. A salsa dance? This should be interesting.

But when Omar spun her into a firm hold then began to sway with her to the beat, his eyes locked on hers, she quickly adjusted her expectations and followed his lead.

Dancing with Briar had been fun; this dance was a taste of heaven. Omar danced the salsa with grace and confidence, Ellie's full skirts swished around her legs and his, and the sultry music seemed to move their bodies with its power. They danced around each other, apart then together, touching and releasing, their eyes locked between spins. Ellie felt as if a lost part of herself had returned, and the sensation was marvelous. Once again, the other dancers circled to watch, clapping and shouting to the rapid beat. And when Omar laid her back over his arm for a spectacular finale, she stared up into his eyes sparkling through his black mask and felt fully alive.

The cheers and applause were even louder this time, and when they straightened, held hands, and took a bow, Ellie realized that every human in the room had gathered to watch that dance. In all her years at Faraway Castle, nothing quite like this had happened before.

But then the band swept into a waltz, and couples rejoined them on the dance floor. Omar gave her a questioning look, and she turned to take his hand and begin. This time they simply waltzed like everyone else, and it was possibly even better. She felt like thistledown in his light clasp, airy and free. His dark eyes studied her face, yet she could not guess his thoughts. Had he learned how to hide his emotions from her? No one but the Gamekeeper—and Briar—had successfully done so before.

"What are you thinking, Omar?" she asked. "You look so . . . intense."

"I am thinking how incredibly beautiful you are," he said in his silky voice, and Ellie's knees nearly melted. "Why did you decide to come tonight?"

She lowered her gaze to his tie. After an uncomfortable moment, she said, "I always wanted to come with you, but I was afraid."

"Afraid? Of me?"

She shook her head decidedly and felt her ponytail swish over her bare shoulders. "Never of you. Of your parents, of your people, of . . . of Madame Genevieve. And a little afraid of myself. There is much you don't know about me, Omar. To be honest, there is much I don't know about myself."

"Isn't that true of most people? We are always discovering who we want to be and who we truly are. Our actions reveal our hearts, and I find your heart even more beautiful than your face."

He had danced her to the side of the dance floor nearest the garden doors. Taking her by the hand, he walked her through the throng of guests and out onto the wide deck. There, beneath the stars, several other couples sat together on the low wall or embraced, oblivious to their surroundings. Omar led Ellie down a set of steps nearly hidden beneath arbors covered in flowering vines and into a narrow garden that bloomed in glowing, magical splendor thanks to Rosa's rare gift. Carnations, phlox, moonflowers, and lilies blended rich scents into a heady perfume. Hand in hand they wandered the garden paths until Omar found an unoccupied bench beneath a vine-draped pergola. He pulled off his mask, laid his jacket on the bench to protect Ellie's gown, then sat beside her.

"Ellie, you already know, but I must tell you again: I have never loved anyone the way I love you. You are everything I most admire. You are strong and independent, yet gentle and generous. You think of other people before yourself and never seem aware of your own beauty and charm. I love watching you with my younger siblings and can easily imagine raising a family with you. You use your magical gifts to benefit others, not yourself; and you even demonstrate love to hobgoblins and brownies, creatures few people notice, let alone befriend."

He paused and swallowed hard. "I ask now if you would consider marrying me and moving to my country. If you would rather that I stay in the north with you, I will do it. I would almost prefer that, particularly during summers. We could return here for holidays, or you could even work here if you like. I believe you should develop and use your magical gifts, and I don't think you would be happy living an idle life. Please say you will think about it, Ellie."

She might have broken into his speech had she been able to find her voice. His loving words had choked her up completely, and now she had to release a gasp like a sob before she could speak. "You are the dearest . . .! Omar, you say the kindest things, but why would you wish to marry a nobody like me? I . . . I round up cinder sprites for a living! You could have any lady or princess at this resort."

"Not one lady or princess at Faraway Castle or anywhere else has ever captured my heart the way you do. I was a lost man from the time you poured lemonade down my back. I had noticed you before then, but only from a distance. Once I looked into your eyes, there was no turning back. You are not a nobody; you are more of a 'somebody' than anyone else I know."

Her heart overflowed with joy. Omar loved her! Wanted to marry her!

Yet reality could not be ignored.

"Your parents will never accept me," she said, her voice breaking. "How could I live with the knowledge that I had separated you from the people you love most? There would come a day when you resented me for it."

He shook his head, taking her hand in his. "Never. Even if it came to that—which I don't believe it will—you are all the family I need. With you I feel more . . . more truly myself than ever before, because you accept me as I am. And I thought—I hoped—you might love me as I am and continue loving me as time passes, even as we grow old together."

Ellie could hardly think. Twice she tried to speak but failed. Omar simply held her hand and wooed her with his eyes. Which was a very effective technique in the soft moonlight.

"Omar, I . . . Marriage is a very serious proposition, especially since your parents disapprove of me. I admit that I . . . I can think only of you . . . Truly I feel as if a moment never passes without my thinking of you, imagining what you would say and how I would answer. I can think of nothing I would like more than to grow old with you." She squeezed his hand and swallowed hard. "You tempt me so!"

She sounded almost angry, but he smiled in response. "I sincerely hope so. Not all temptation is evil, you know." He lifted her hand to his lips and kissed her fingers. "You needn't give me a promise tonight. I don't want to pressure you into a decision you will later regret. Come to me freely or not at all, my dear."

She nodded and gulped again.

"But may I think of you as my girlfriend, for lack of a better term?"

Again Ellie's heart seemed to swell in her chest, restricting her breathing. She gave a short nod before she could think of possible consequences.

He sucked in a shaky breath and sat back on the bench, then blew a few breaths in and out. "Thank you," he said so quietly that she might have missed it had she not been watching him. "This is more than I dared hope for!"

Ellie could not imagine why he would feel so nervous and concerned. She was the one being honored beyond reason!

"May I tell my parents that we are . . . seeing each other?" he asked. "They will need time to adjust to the idea. I sincerely believe they will love you once they get to know you, just as the children do. I suspect my mother has already been considering the idea, and my father has a tender heart beneath all his adherence to tradition."

Even the mention of his mother sent a flood of apprehension over Ellie. She didn't think she could bear it if the gentle queen were to look upon her with disapproval. But when Omar rose and extended his hand to her, she took it and gave him a quivering smile. In the moonlight he could not see her expression clearly, but he must have felt the tremors in her hand, for he looped it through his arm and pressed it close to his side. "Ellie Calmer," he said in a meditative tone. "My girl. My intended."

Ellie melted all over again at the sound of her name in his charming accent. They returned to the castle at a quick pace, hardly noticing the night's beauty, so absorbed were they in contemplation of the future. As they climbed the deck stairs, Ellie glanced up at Omar, and his smile nearly blinded her.

Just as they approached the ballroom door, Ellie heard a terrible crash followed by screams, shouts, and a general panic near the buffet tables. A wave of panicked people, male and female, flooded the dance floor, caught up the dancers in its current, backed up around the doors, then began to pour outside, still shouting in horror.

Ellie heard snatches as people rushed past: ". . . hideous!" ". . . crawling all over the floor!" ". . . cake and pie and . . ." ". . . thousands of them!" ". . . never believed the rumors, but . . ."

"Oh no!" she moaned. "Geraldo!"

CHAPTER NINETEEN

LLIE LET GO OF OMAR'S HAND, RUSHED TO THE side of the deck, climbed over, and jumped to the ground three feet below, heedless of her rustling gown. From there she dashed to the service door, opened it with a wave of her hand, and began to work her way around the outside of the room toward the buffet.

A frightful sight met her eyes as the tables came in sight. One had collapsed, and it and the surrounding floor were covered in small humanoids swarming like rats over pies and cakes, slipping and falling in the mess, and fighting tooth-and-nail for the most delectable selections. She spotted Geraldo atop a flattened chocolate cake, beating off competitors with butter knife and fork.

Around this pitched battle scurried brownies wringing their hands over the chaos, desperately trying to clean up the mess but beaten back by hobgoblins protecting their booty. Ellie paused to catch her breath. Her spray bottle was in her backpack . . . somewhere. But on this night when she felt magic flowing through her veins, just maybe she could resolve the situation with her voice alone. She had to try.

Fixing her gaze on Geraldo first, then letting it drift from one hobgoblin to another, she spoke in a calming tone. "My friends, you know that theft and disturbance are not allowed in the castle where you live so comfortably. You have deliberately shown yourselves to guests, which is also strictly forbidden. Do you truly want to find yourselves evicted and sent away? Stop quarreling at once and help the brownies clean up the mess you've made, and I will do my best to calm the humans and make them forget this disaster."

When she first began to speak, Geraldo dropped his weapons and shoved his fingers into his big ears. The others also tried to ignore her. But she firmed her tone and injected more power into her voice, and one by one they stopped quarreling. By the time she spoke the last sentence, every hobgoblin looked up at her with sheepish expression and sorrowful eyes. Geraldo held out longest, but at last he hung his head. "I am sorry, Miss Ellie and Madame Director." His withered chest rose and fell in a sigh. "We will help clean up the mess."

Only then did Ellie realize that Madame Genevieve stood behind her, observing all. Her grim, accusing expression might have intimidated Ellie at another time, but just now she still had work to do. She was uncertain how long the hobgoblins' change of heart would last, so she hovered nearby during the clean-up. The ugly little creatures proved true to their word, and between brownies and hobgoblins, the floor was spotless in amazingly short order.

"Great work, Marielle. We'll help them remove the heavy items," Briar paused to say in her ear. Ellie blinked, but he moved away before she could question him.

She heard Omar say to Briar, "I didn't know

the little people could be seen if they chose. Remarkable!"

Little did he know how disastrous this could be for the resort, and for Ellie herself. If she couldn't calm the non-magical guests, they might leave Faraway Castle in horror and never return—and she would quickly be out of a job.

Omar and Briar set a sack of shattered china on top of the broken table, then lifted it between them and carried it out of the ballroom. The brownies cleaned and straightened everything behind them, and soon no evidence of the catastrophe remained.

Except for the confused humans milling like sheep in the ballroom and gardens. They seemed dazed, Ellie thought as she surveyed the room. They had heard her voice while she spoke to the hobgoblins, but although their panic had ended, they were still cowed and fearful. Had she caused this? If so, she didn't know how.

Ellie threaded her way between guests to the garden doors, which seemed the best place for projecting her voice to everyone in the gardens as well as the ballroom. Again she took a few deep breaths and focused. "There is no need to fear; all is well." She felt her magic wind its way about the room as she spoke. "Some greedy little ones tried to steal the cakes and pies while no one was looking, but they have apologized, and the mess is cleaned up. Nothing important happened. Set your minds at rest, forget your fear, and enjoy this amazing Summer Ball!"

Nearby, people blinked and looked around at each other, their faces brightening into happiness and anticipation. The band members picked up their instruments, laughing at themselves for panicking over nothing, and their leader started them out on a lively polka. Several couples began to dance. To Ellie's surprise, Omar's parents were among them.

Just as she turned to see if Omar had returned, a sharp voice cut through the music and the buzz of conversation. "That girl in the purple gown, there by the door—it's that cinder-sprite girl! It's Cinder Ellie! How dare she come to the ball! She is part of the staff, a hired servant!"

It was Lady Raquel, her haughty face twisted with disgust, one perfectly manicured finger pointed directly at Ellie. People nearby turned to stare, some confused, others shocked, a few offended.

While Ellie stood frozen, Lady Gillian stepped forward and ripped the mask off her face. "Imposter!" she shouted. "I know how you've been stalking Prince Omar, and now everyone will know the truth about you."

Other voices rose in accusation and protest. No one knew that Ellie had just saved the party, for all memory of the incident was now gone. How had she managed to remove their memory? Would she be in trouble for using her power to meddle with people's minds?

And then Madame Genevieve appeared beside her. Although she stood near to Ellie, she spoke in a carrying tone for all to hear: "Ellie Calmer, your position here at Faraway Castle Resort is hereby terminated. You have abused your position, broken many rules, neglected your responsibilities in pursuit of personal advancement, and used magic in excessive and unlawful ways. You must pack your possessions and leave the grounds at once, or I will summon the proper authorities." Her voice held vindictive satisfaction.

Why did this woman hate her so? Ellie wondered.

All around her she saw accusing faces, expressions of shock and condemnation. Where was Omar? Nowhere in sight. Would he condemn her too?

Horror and humiliation smothered any defense she might have made. She turned, pushed and shoved her way outside, and ran down the deck steps leading toward the side garden gate. Just as she reached the ground, she stumbled and one of her slippers fell off. But she ran onward, hopping and limping, until she reached the gate. Only when safely on the service road did she stop to pull off the other shoe before limping to her cottage. Once inside her house, she leaned her back against the door, dropped the slipper, slid down to sit on the floor, covered her face with both hands, and tried to process events of the past hour.

The Gamekeeper's final words echoed in her mind: "I ask only that you allow nothing to destroy your joy tonight." But how could he have anticipated such a calamity as this?

Omar and Briar carried the table outside, dumped

the sack of broken plates into a garbage bin, then left the table propped outside a shed for later repair. The yard was dark, for none of the festive lighting extended to such practical places. "That was exciting," Briar commented dryly. "Ellie's power is impressive, but she needs further training to control it properly. Tell me, Omar, is there magic in your family?"

Omar glanced up, brushing off his hands, but Briar's face was too shadowed to read. "Why do you ask?"

"I've noticed a few things," Briar replied. "You're able to see magical creatures that normally hide themselves from humans."

"That started after I chased Tor to the island. I first saw brownies and hobgoblins in the dining room, and then brownies in the stable. I even met a toadstool fairy. Everyone can see cinder sprites, unicorns, and the lake serpent, can't they?"

Briar opened the side door and motioned for Omar to enter the Castle. "Most people, at most times. Where magic is concerned, it's dangerous to generalize. More to the point, I believe it is safe to say that a siren spoke to you while you were on the island."

"I don't recall it." Omar frowned. "Do you think the siren blocked my memory of talking with her?"

"No doubt. Sirens seem to be adept at manipulating memories." Briar again waved Omar inside.

Omar stepped through the doorway but turned back to address the other prince. "You have magic, don't you? I can sense it, just as I sometimes sense Ellie's."

"Yeah, I have some. My sister and I both inherited magic from our mother." Briar gave Omar an amused grin and held up his hands. "I need to wash before we return to the ballroom. I have an announcement to make tonight."

On the way to the washroom, Omar remarked, "I didn't know you had a sister." He rolled up his sleeves, turned on the warm tap, and scrubbed stickiness and dirt from his hands. His tuxedo would need dry-cleaning after tonight, for certain.

Briar concentrated on washing his hands. "Most people don't."

Omar detected strange undertones in the prince's voice. "Why not? What are you not telling me?"

Briar looked him straight in the eyes, paused,

then grinned. "I was going to wait and make you find out along with everyone else, but I can't do it. Here's the deal: I've spent time with Ellie this week, trying to get to know her. I can't help being proud of the woman she has become. Omar, if you were jealous when I danced with her tonight, don't be. I love Ellie, but not in the same way you do."

Omar's brain processed this speech. "You're telling me Ellie is your sister."

"Never underestimate a mathematician," Briar said. "She is. My twin. My *older* twin, to be exact. And now, should you return to the ballroom with me, you will soon hear the story—or as much of it as I know—of how she came to be here at Faraway Castle. As soon as I was positive that Ellie is indeed Crown Princess Marielle Yvette of Auvers, I sent for our parents. I'm not sure when they will arrive, but it will happen in the next day or two."

The two young men faced off in the washroom off the kitchen, strange surroundings for a revelation. Omar knew he was blinking and staring like an idiot, but he couldn't help himself. "Ellie is a princess. I should have known all along."

Briar shrugged one shoulder. "How could you

have known? Many exceptional women are not princesses, or even noblewomen in the sense the word is commonly used." He sounded slightly annoyed. "But you are missing the crucial point of my revelation: Ellie will be queen someday. The law of primogeniture in Auvers includes firstborn daughters."

Omar's brow wrinkled. "That will certainly come as a surprise to her. How do you feel about becoming second in line for the throne after being the crown prince all your life?"

"Not all my life, only since Ellie disappeared. And, to be frank, I feel free!" The lift of one brow added a sardonic twist to this statement, leaving Omar confused.

"Shall we return to the ballroom?" Briar suggested. "I ask only that you allow me to break the news to Marielle. I believe her memories are starting to return. She danced with me tonight as if we were both still seven, performing our old lifts and spins."

Omar might have remarked that she had danced just as naturally with him, but he kept that knowledge to himself, sensing Briar needed this connection with his twin sister.

The band still played as they entered, but dancers on the floor had stopped. People clustered at the garden doors, others turned to see what was happening, and the music faltered as band members dropped out one by one. Whispers became murmurs, and soon the room buzzed with talk.

Had the hobgoblins caused more trouble? Where was Ellie?

"What's happening?" Omar asked a young lord he often teamed up with for tennis matches.

Lord Carevo, better known as Dino, answered, "Raquel and Gillian unmasked a staff member who dressed up and pretended to be a guest—the hot blonde you danced with. Did you know? The director fired her right in front of everyone."

But Omar was no longer listening. He ran toward the garden door and struggled to break through the crowd. Ellie must have run outside, for everyone still stared in that direction. "Ellie!" he called.

At that moment, what felt like a cushion of magic dropped over the entire company, muting all sound. As Omar slowly turned, feeling as if he moved in a dream, a familiar voice called for attention. Prince Briar stood on the dais, his hands raised.

"Some" magic? Right.

Every eye in the room focused on Briar. "I wish to tell you a story." His voice penetrated the thick silence. "Some of you know parts of this tale but not all. Eleven years ago, the royal family of Auvers traveled toward Faraway Castle, intending to experience our first family holiday. On the way, my parents, my twin sister, and I took a side trip to see the spectacular mountain views. One of the vehicles in our convoy got a flat tire, so my family stopped to picnic and enjoy the scenery while servants changed the flat. While we were eating, Marielle jumped up and chased after some bird or creature she had seen, calling for me to follow. By the time I got up and chased after her, it was too late. Not that I would have been able to save her.

"A huge griffin dropped out of the sky, grabbed Marielle from behind by her arms, and carried her away, high into the sky and beyond our sight. Our guards could not shoot at it for fear of harming Marielle, and the creature was quickly too far away for my mother's magic to reach."

Omar listened, as spellbound as everyone

around him, while Briar spun out his astonishing tale.

"Our parents ordered an extensive search throughout the surrounding region, but no word of a little golden-haired girl could be found. They paid hunting parties to find that griffin. Our mother, Queen Brigitte, hired magicians to locate it or Marielle. All for nothing. It was as if she had vanished from the earth. As years passed with no sign of her, even our parents began to accept that she was forever lost to us and gave her up for dead, but I knew she must be alive and searched for her on my own.

"This summer I decided to visit Faraway Castle for the first time, and almost on the day I arrived I noticed a young woman bearing a strong resemblance to my family—to me, for that matter. I investigated, learned of her magical ability of persuasive speech and her connection with magical creatures, and my suspicion became certainty. Not until I conversed with a personage who professed to know her herbwoman protector did I discover when and how my sister disappeared eleven years ago: My father's men were unable to locate her because the herbwoman places strong protective boundaries around her home."

Briar paused to allow this information to sink into his audience's minds, then pronounced: "The young woman known as Ellie Calmer, Controller of Magical Creatures at Faraway Castle, is my twin sister, Marielle Yvette Toulouse, daughter of Queen Brigitte and her consort, Prince Francis. She is my *older* sister, and rightfully Crown Princess of Auvers."

The magical restraint lifted. Gasps and murmurs filled the room. Briar jumped off the platform near Lady Raquel and the Honorable Gillian. "Ladies," he said coolly in passing, but it was enough.

Lady Raquel's face was livid, her lips compressed. Gillian moaned, "The lost princess Marielle! We insulted our own Crown Princess! But how could we have known? We thought she was dead! It isn't fair!"

The conquering prince passed Omar with only a twinkling glance then approached the king and queen of Khenifra. He bowed low before them— Omar could find no fault with Prince Briar's manner. He was respectful without subservience, and his face was, for once, devoid of humor.

"Your Majesties, I ask you now, as brother to the Crown Princess Marielle, if you will accept her as a worthy bride for your son Prince Omar."

Omar swallowed hard.

King Aryn tipped his chin down and nearly smiled. "Your Highness, we had already discussed the matter and decided to accept our son's choice of wife, whatever her station in life. Your sister has already proven herself a worthy consort to any man with intelligence and spirit enough to claim her heart. Someday she will be a wise and just queen."

Queen Sofia smiled directly at Omar. "Go to her, Omar. She needs you."

Briar also turned to face Omar, pointed toward the garden door, and stated with evident enjoyment: "She went that way."

Omar rushed from the ballroom, his heart flying ahead of his feet.

CHAPTER TWENTY

LLIE SAT THERE IN THE DARKNESS WITH HER back against the door, staring into space while questions whirled through her head.

Why would the Gamekeeper tell her not to lose her joy, no matter what? Did he know something she didn't know? Did the director have authority to fire her, or should she contact him?

"Enough self-pity," Ellie growled. "One way or another, I've got to get out of this dress."

She pushed herself to her feet, took two steps, tripped over something, and staggered a few paces, certain she was going to ruin her gorgeous gown. But the dress was tougher than it appeared, and she managed to find her balance and a light switch.

She'd tripped over her backpack on the floor just inside the tiny living room. Someone must have . . . The mind-picture of that horrid pooka in her cottage flashed through her thoughts, but before she could creep herself out entirely, a chorus of squeaks distracted her. A little creature dashed from under one chair to another. She recognized that gleaming white fur. "Frosti? How . . .?" Two more sprites poked their heads from beneath the little sofa and whistled—the boys! Then Sparki scampered directly to Ellie and disappeared beneath her skirts. "Wait, did you . . .? No, you can't possibly have carried in my pack. Why are you still here? Is the coach somewhere outside?"

Even as she asked the question, she knew the coach was gone. The Gamekeeper would have to come back for these four. "I need to set up cages for you girls and your friends. Would you fellows like to have names?"

She gathered the impression that names would be welcome, but she was fresh out of ideas. "Maybe I will find a way to ask the children to name you. I hope they're able to come say goodbye."

More to the point, would Omar come? Of course he would. But what could he say or do to make a future together possible?

No, best to focus on the current situation. She sat on the edge of a chair in a puddle of frothy skirts, leaned her elbows on her knees, and focused on Frosti and Sparki, who stepped out in the open to inform her. Their little mouths worked and their slender horns bobbed as they earnestly squeaked their news. And as she listened, Ellie caught the drift of their meaning. Really, she must find a way to learn cinder sprite language.

"You want to stay with me?" she responded to a particularly impassioned speech, jumbled though it was, since both sprites talked at once. "And the boys too? But, girls, I've been dismissed from my position here and must leave the resort immediately."

All four chorused in protest, and she completely lost the sense in their response. Hearing something about the Gamekeeper, she said, "This isn't your fault or the Gamekeeper's in any way. I chose to take the risk in attending the ball, and up until Geraldo—he's a hobgoblin—caused a disaster at the buffet tables, everything was wonderful. I danced with Omar, and . . ."

Her voice gave out. She shook her head, lips compressed, trying to regain control. Memories of the evening flitted through her thoughts, including her dance with Briar. Strange, how dancing with him had seemed familiar.

"And he called me . . . Marielle," she said.

Memories tumbled through her thoughts so quickly that she felt dizzy. "That is my name—Marielle. Briar is the boy I danced with all those years ago. Now I remember his face back then, and I know. He . . . he always found fault with my dancing and picked on me. But if anyone else criticized me, he sprang to my defense."

Her eyes widened to the shape of saucers. "Briar is my twin brother," she whispered. "And he knows!" she said aloud. "That rat, he knows! Why didn't he tell me?"

The sprites scampered away, still chirping to each other, as she awkwardly stood up, trying not to step on her skirts. "Omar!" she whispered. "I must tell him!"

At that moment she heard a knock at the door

and Omar's voice. "Ellie? I know you're in there. Please open the door. I have important news— good news—to share!" She spun around, nearly fell upon the door in her rush to open it, then jerked it wide open.

He stood there, his expression hopeful, tentative, concerned. Then he held out a sparkling glass slipper. "Might this be yours, my lady?"

She laughed in a nervous burst and snatched it from him with both hands. Unable to hold everything back, she exclaimed in a rush, dancing in place with excitement: "Omar! Everything has changed! I remember! I know who I am! When Briar called me Marielle—did you hear him?—I didn't even notice at first. I knew it was my name without thinking. When we danced, it felt so natural, as if we had done it a thousand times— which we have! And just now I realized that he's my brother! My twin brother who tormented the life out of me, but he was my best friend. No wonder I always felt so comfortable with him and never mistook his friendliness for flirting."

Only then did she notice Omar's lack of surprise. "Did you know already?"

"Briar just told everyone at the ball that you

are his sister, Crown Princess Marielle. He explained how you were carried off by a griffin, and how, after years of desperate searching, your parents believed you were dead. But they, your parents, are coming here soon, perhaps tomorrow!"

Ellie listened with the slipper clutched against her chest, breathing hard. Then, with a gasp, she dropped the shoe, which hit the floor with a loud clunk. Covering her face with her hands, she shook her head. "It's too much to take in! Omar, what shall I do?"

"I have a great idea," he said, only partly joking. "You should marry me. May I ask you now?

She parted her hands to give him a glowing smile . . . and nodded.

Omar went down on one knee right there on her doorstep. "Marielle—my dearest Ellie—will you marry me? Please be my wife!"

He looked so hopeful and sweet and uncertain that Ellie bent down, took his face between her hands, and kissed him. "Yes! Oh yes, I will marry you, Omar!"

He stared up at her, dazed and startled, though

he appeared not at all displeased.

Ellie stood up straight, took a step back inside, and laughed again. "My first kiss, and I stole it!"

He blinked, stood up, swallowed hard, then grinned sheepishly. "It was my first kiss too. And I didn't mind having it stolen. Not at all." He stepped forward, took her in his arms, and said, "But I'm stealing the next one." And he proceeded to kiss her thoroughly right there in the doorway, making up for lost time.

After a few minutes, Ellie pulled back slightly and blurted, "But this changes everything. Now I must become queen someday, unless I abdicate and let Briar be king. And what will your parents think? They might accept me now, but I hate to think I'm acceptable only for my rank."

He nodded soberly. "I suppose we can never know for certain, but my father told me, only minutes ago, that they had already decided to allow me to marry whomever I chose, and I believe them. They understand that their own happiness in an arranged marriage is a rare blessing and . . . well, while you and I danced, I saw my mother watching us, and she looked pleased, like the cat who stole the cream. I didn't stop to analyze at the time, but now I think I understand: She recognized love when she saw us together."

"Then we are officially engaged to marry," Ellie said in wonder, gazing up at him. "Omar, I have loved you for so long! I want to marry you soon. I don't want to be apart while you finish school. After tonight, I don't think I could be comfortable working at the resort even if Madame would take me back."

He smiled in mild amusement. "I expect you will travel to Auvers with your parents and spend the next few months learning how to be Crown Princess. Your life is about to change in major ways, my sweet Ellie." He placed one hand on her cheek and kissed her forehead.

"I know, and that frightens me." She turned her face into his caress, sighed, then slid her arms up around his neck and pressed close. "The only change I really want is to be with you all the time."

"I want that too." He rested his cheek on her hair and sighed. "But many other changes must come first. We could elope, but I don't want to alienate your parents from the start."

Ellie sighed. "You are right, of course. I hope Briar comes along to help me adjust to Auvers. I have some memories of it, but I'm sure it will look entirely different to me now."

They held each other for a long moment, soaking in the closeness. But Ellie's brain could not relax. "Are you sure you want to be prince consort someday? You're already a prince, so you won't need a new title—that's good. I don't remember my parents well enough to know what it's like for my father. I seem to remember my mother being rather . . . forceful. And that frightens me too. What if she objects to our marriage?"

"Ellie, don't borrow trouble. Let's meet them first, tell them of our betrothal, and see where things go from there. I'm sure objections and impediments will come, but we'll handle things together, all right? Being prince consort will be a challenging adventure, true, but I already expected adventure in marrying you. You'll make a great queen someday."

"Do you really think so?"

"I know so." He held her close, and she relaxed against him, though he could almost feel the tumult of her thinking.

"Do I hear cinder sprites?" Omar asked after a

moment. "I thought the Gamekeeper came to take them."

Ellie tipped her face up and smiled. "You do, and he did, but some decided to come back. I have so much to tell you about my visit to the Gamekeeper's house and how I was able to come to the ball! I even met the griffin that stole me. That was the weirdest part of a very strange day."

She paused, grimaced, and shuddered. "I think I was happier not remembering some of my past. But most of today was incredibly good. And I am so exhausted I can hardly think straight."

She rose on tiptoe and regarded him earnestly. "Omar, will you mind terribly if I keep a few cinder sprites around our house? They won't start fires or stink of sulphur, I promise."

He laughed, quickly kissed her again, unable to resist, then answered, "My poor brain is galloping all-out, trying to keep up with your train of thought. And I suppose having magical creatures around the house comes with marrying a magical-creature wrangler. Credit where credit is due: I might never have worked up nerve to speak to you if a sprite hadn't lured you into my bedchamber."

Laughing, Ellie hid her face in his shoulder.

"What a crazy story to tell!"

"If we don't spread it, my little brothers will." Grinning, he said, "The children will be beyond delighted to have you in the family, Ellie! We do need to return to the ballroom and let everyone know."

She smoothed the back of his hair and sighed. "I know, but it was lovely to stretch out this time together, just the two of us."

"The first of many times," he said with manifest satisfaction.

Ellie ran to fix her hair and makeup, donned the glass slippers, then returned in a rush to take Omar's arm and walk back to the castle. They entered the lobby through the main doors, and their entrance caused a stir. Rafiq, Yasmine, Karim, and Rita rushed to surround them before they were halfway to the ballroom door.

"We heard the news! Ellie is a princess!" "You two can get married now, right?" "Ellie will be our sister!" "Did you kiss her yet?" All four Zeidans talked at once, and not until Ellie bent to kiss each one in turn did they settle down.

"Yes, darlings, we are going to get married, and you are the first to officially know," she told them quietly. "And you will be my brothers and sisters forever and ever."

Rita and Karim hopped around, squealing and waving their arms. Yasmine clasped her hands beneath her chin and beamed for joy, bouncing on her toes. Rafiq shuffled his feet, his expression shifting from a smile to a frown to a smile with dizzying rapidity until it finally settled into satisfied lines and remained. "Good going, Omar. You finally got her."

Ellie took Rita and Karim by the hands, and the six of them entered the ballroom together, all glowing with happiness.

King Aryn and Queen Sofia hurried forward to meet them. The king glanced back and forth between their faces and smiled. "It is settled, then."

Omar's mother faced Ellie squarely. "I hope you may someday forgive our behavior toward you, my dear. We gladly welcome you into our family and our hearts, and I only wish we had revealed our change of heart before your heritage was made known to us. May we"—she glanced from Ellie to Omar and back—"announce your betrothal tonight?

Ellie let go of the children's hands and reached both hands to the Queen, who grasped them quickly. "I forgive you freely, Your Majesties, and you have my permission to tell the whole world!"

Any remaining fear or resentment slipped away when she saw the genuine joy in Omar's face, as well as the relief and pleasure so evident in his parents' smiles. Word was sent to the band, which interrupted its song and played a flourish to demand attention.

Then King Arryn and Queen Sofia stood on the platform together, smiling from ear to ear—a very handsome couple, Ellie thought once again—and the King proclaimed: "Tonight we ask you all to share our joy in announcing the betrothal of our son Omar Jibran Tazim Zeidan, Prince of Khenifra, to Marielle Yvette Toulouse, Crown Princess of Auvers."

A great cheer arose, for the capricious crowd delighted in the tale of a lost princess found and had already forgotten its condemnation of an hour before. First to congratulate them was Prince Briar, who embraced his sister and spoke into her ear: "He will spoil you with kindness, but as your brother I am bound to keep you humble and cross."

"Like old times," Ellie said, and kissed his cheek. "I remember more about your peskiness now and promise to screech insults at you regularly."

He gazed fondly into her eyes. "Some things never change."

She hugged him again. "Thank you, Briar. For everything." Then she remembered. "But . . . the throne? Do you mind very much?"

He laughed softly. "Marielle, why do you think I have searched for you so diligently all these years? Aside from the minor fact that I missed you, I mean. Becoming heir apparent to the throne was the worst thing that ever happened to me. I have no desire whatsoever to be king."

Ellie had to laugh. "And you think I want to be queen? All because I was born a few minutes before you? You are soooo lucky Auvers doesn't demand a male heir to the throne."

"If it did, neither of us would be heir, since our mother wouldn't be queen."

"There is that," Ellie agreed. "I suppose I'll just have to accept my role, which won't be so bad with Omar at my side." She looked proudly at her fiancé, who was now a few paces away, accepting congratulations from a crowd of friends.

Briar gave her his usual wry smile. "You two are a great match. Confronting Mother is not my favorite thing, but I promise to stand with you during your transition. And I'm one-hundred percent behind Omar. It's a good thing you two are officially betrothed."

"You think Mother will object?"

His amused expression told her much. "I merely advise you to prepare for the worst. Only you have the right to choose your husband, and you have chosen well. Omar may not have magic, but he has a strong backbone. He'll handle the pressure. You're the one I worry about, soft-hearted as you are. Mother will use that and your sense of obligation against you."

Ellie appreciated her brother's honesty. He didn't even try to soothe her with magic, which she appreciated. "Thank you," she said. "Thank you for everything, Briar."

He accepted her quick hug with a brief smile. "Yeah, yeah. I'm doing it for myself too. You'll notice, the director discreetly disappeared, poor old thing. And your magical friends are gathered to celebrate with you. Now go dance with your fiancé."

The band began to play a romantic song, and several couples took to the floor. Omar turned, caught Ellie's gaze, and raised his brows. She hurried to take his hand, and they joined the dancers, moving cheek to cheek. Ellie was tickled to see, moments later, the King and Queen of Khenifra dancing nearby.

Even as she relaxed into Omar's arms, Ellie noticed faces in the crowd surrounding the dance floor. Four dwarfs, her particular friends Chuck, Tasha, Sten, and Nillie, all wearing their glamours, stood at the edge of the dance floor and smiled their approval.

"It's a wonderful party," Ellie told Nillie, the resort's event-planner, as she and Omar danced past, and all four dwarfs gave her two thumbs-ups.

Sira and other brownies had worked their way to the front of the throng and waved to her and Omar with evident delight despite their mournful faces. Even Geraldo perched on the edge of the band platform and glowered at her, his twiggy arms crossed over his chest. She winked at him, and he rolled his eyes, which made her smile.

Ellie could only imagine how pleased her cinder sprite friends would be to hear her news, and the Gamekeeper, who had orchestrated this entire evening, she appreciated most of all.

"Omar, I do not see how I could ever be happier!" she murmured into his ear.

His arms around her tightened briefly, and she heard a smile in his voice as he replied, "Oh, I think we'll find a way."

But wait! What about Tor and his siren? Whatever happened to those two? Find out in J.M. Stengl's upcoming novel—

THE SIREN AND THE SCHOLAR

A Little Mermaid Romance

Meanwhile don't miss out on this wonderful prequel novella introducing Kammy and Tor.

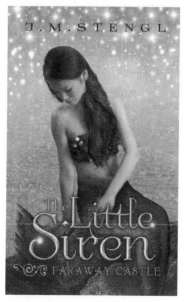

Visit www.JMStengl.com *to get your free copy.*

ABOUT THE AUTHOR

J.M. STENGL IS A NATIVE OF SOUTHERN CALIFORNIA WHO, after a whirlwind life as a military wife, now makes her home with her husband in North Carolina, where she serves at the beck and call of two purebred cats and one adorable grand-daughter. Obsessions include all things animal rescue, fairy-tale romances, knowing the lyrics to the best songs from old musicals, and perfecting the perfect pastry crust.

During her former career as a historical romance novelist, Stengl won both the Carol Award and RWA's Inspirational Readers' Choice Award. Now she prefers her novels to include a dash of magic along with the heart-melting romance.

Visit her website at www.JMStengl.com

Made in the USA
Middletown, DE
30 March 2018